MURDER IN CASCADE

AN ELLEN DOUGLAS MYSTERY

JILL BROWN

Leucocholy Press

To Rick, who's encouragement made this happen.

Chapter One

It was a dark and stormy night. At least, it should have been if the stories were true and the atmosphere somehow sensed that something ominous was coming. Instead, it was a beautiful, crisp fall day, with the sun shining on leaves that had turned vivid shades of yellow, orange, and red. It was just cold enough to require a sweatshirt outside. I put my American Bulldog/Shar-Pei mix, Louisa, in the car to head to town for a walk, and then ran back into the house to grab one.

Going for a walk was part of my new "get healthy" routine. After becoming a widow in my early forties, I focused entirely on my only child and my career. But she had just moved out to an apartment closer to her college, and I'd decided it was time to work on being more active while I figured out what I wanted to do with the rest of my life. I'd had a career for the last thirty years, but I'd been on my way to being burned out, so when they offered me an "early out," I decided to retire. Now that I no longer had to worry about adjusting my routine to Noelle's schedule and I wasn't locked into my demanding job, I was thinking it might be time to try one of those paths

I didn't take when I was younger. The road not taken, so to speak. Just wasn't sure yet what road that would be.

Louisa loved that I'd started taking her for more walks, too. Every time I grabbed my tennis shoes, she started quivering with excitement. We had several places we went, but our favorite was Cascade Falls Park. It was the centerpiece of my little Midwestern town of Cascade – Population 4000. On any given day, you would find many of the town's residents there at the Pop Warner football fields, baseball/softball complex, the disc golf course, the picnic area, or the playground. We were headed to the trails that wound through the woods between the railroad embankment, the creek, and the town cemetery.

I parked, grabbed a water bottle and Louisa's collapsible bowl, and then we headed across the bridge to the trailhead just beyond it. I was hoping to do at least two and a half miles, so I urged my dog to pick up the pace. The air was crisp and cool with the scent of decaying leaves, damp wood, and a hint of evergreen. As we walked, I was sad to see the number of fallen trees that were lying along the paths. A tornado had gone through a few months ago, and the forest still showed signs of it. Many trees that hadn't fallen completely showed signs of damage, with broken limbs hanging by a thread. What was so strange was that many of these branches were still covered in soft leaves, with very little browning at the edges, as if they were still attached to a healthy plant.

Lou loved this walk because there were lots of squirrels, chipmunks, and birds for her to try to chase, so I had my work cut out for me keeping her from yanking the leash from my wrist. She was a muscular sixty-pound dog, and I barely acknowledged that gyms existed. So, when she wanted to chase one of the friendly neighborhood wildlife, I had a hard time keeping her from taking me with her. We stopped at a fork in the trail so I could give her some water, and I noticed what looked like a large limb across the trail in the direction we wanted to go.

I wonder when that fell! I hope we can get around it...

One fork took you to another parking area, which was more of a paved path. The trail I wanted to take was gravel and dirt, with dense foliage on one side and a sharp drop-off to the creek on the other. This part of the forest was not as affected by the recent tornado, and I hadn't seen any other downed limbs along this section of the path before, but I supposed one could have fallen for another reason. If the fallen branch was blocking the whole trail, we would have to take the other fork or turn back around and return the way we'd come. We would miss the part of the trail that had a bridge over the falls.

Our falls was my favorite place in the whole world. I loved standing on the bridge and looking down at the water. It wasn't Niagara, but it was big enough to drown out the outside world when you were contemplating the tragedies in your life. I'd sought solace from a broken heart, mourned loved ones, and prayed over major decisions there ever since I was a teenager. I often paused there on our walks now to say a prayer about what I should do with the rest of my life. I had worked and supported Noelle's activities for so long, I wasn't really sure who I wanted to be. I was just in my early 50s, so I wasn't ready to do nothing. But I also didn't want to go back to an office. I'd been considering my options for a few months now, but I wasn't any closer to making a decision. I really didn't want to miss my prayer time at the falls, so when Lou finished drinking her fill, I decided to see if I could pick my way through the branches and continue our walk.

As I got closer, I saw that the limb was about twelve to eighteen inches in diameter and six or seven feet long. It covered the whole width of the trail. Several smaller limbs were sprouting out from each side. The leaves were just starting to curl on the edges, and I said to Lou, "This didn't fall very long ago." My blood ran cold at what might have happened if I hadn't gone back for my sweatshirt.

Just as I had that thought, Louisa pulled violently on the leash. It was so unexpected, and I was so distracted, that she had pulled the leash completely off my wrist before I could react. "Louisa! *No!*" I shouted as I made a grab for her, but she had leaped over the branch and was already out of reach. Suddenly, she stopped and started whining and then lay down on the ground as close to the tree as she could get.

"What on earth has gotten into you?" I worked my way through the branches to try to get to her. I felt a shiver down my back, as if someone had walked over my grave. I slowed my steps, suddenly not sure I wanted to see what had caused Louisa to be so upset. What I saw froze me in place.

I could see a long blonde ponytail and a leg covered in black capri leggings with cutouts in the legs, ending with a colorful running shoe sticking out from under the tree branch. It was a woman! I couldn't see any blood from the angle I was at, so I rushed forward to see if I could help.

I started calling out, "Are you okay?" as I tried to figure out how I could get to her without hurting her worse. She was almost completely covered by the branch and leaves, so I couldn't really tell what specifically was wrong. There was no answer, but I kept trying to talk to her. "Can you move at all?"

There was something familiar about that ponytail, but I couldn't see her face yet because of all the debris. I finally decided to climb over the main log and see if I could get to her from that side.

I couldn't go around the limb without falling into the creek or pushing through a thicket that had some sharp thorns, so I moved as far to the creek side of the trail as I could before I tried to get over the main branch. I was only five feet tall and hadn't been active for all that long. I wasn't going to be able to just jump over something of this size. I was going to have to either straddle it or step up onto it. I was afraid either would put pressure on the woman lying under it, so I decided I'd better just call for help.

I pulled out my phone and dialed 9-1-1. While we waited for help, I continued to try to get the woman to talk to me, but to no avail. I desperately hoped she would be okay, but it worried me that she hadn't responded to me at all. I knew that being struck in the head with something as large as this tree branch could cause a traumatic brain injury or crush someone, causing internal injuries. I prayed she had just been knocked unconscious and that she would be all right.

Louisa came and rubbed up against my side. I stroked her fur while I listened for sirens to indicate help was on the way. She was still whining softly, and as I looked down to check on her, I realized she had something in her mouth. "What have you got there, Louisa?" I pulled a soggy piece of paper from her mouth and absently stuck it in my pocket.

I looked around at the surrounding trees and tried to figure out if any of the others were about to lose a branch. I knew they said lightning didn't strike twice in the same place, but I wasn't sure if that was true of forests or not. The strange thing was that I didn't really see any in this area that showed damage. It seemed like there should have been a gash, missing bark, or something to indicate that the branch had fallen. Maybe it was just too high for me to see it.

I heard what sounded like someone running up the path behind me and stood to flag them down. "Over here! She's under this branch! I've tried to talk to her, but she hasn't responded."

The emergency crew brushed past me and began assessing the best way to get to the victim. "Please stand back, ma'am," one paramedic said. "We're going to try to lift this off her so we can assess the extent of the injuries."

I firmly gripped Lou's leash and pulled her away, but turned back around when I heard a gasp behind me. They had lifted the tree branch off, and it was clear that the medics were not going to be helping this victim. I was just close enough once the limb was moved to see that her eyes were open and unblinking as she stared at the sky from where she had fallen onto her back.

Oh no!

My vision started to blur...

Chapter Two

When I came to, I was leaning up against a tree with Louisa's cold nose pressed into my hand and a blood pressure cuff on my arm. I couldn't keep from glancing over to where the body was, but my view was blocked by a swarm of officers and techs who were snapping pictures and searching the area. Yellow crime scene tape had been draped around trees, effectively blocking the path and the woods surrounding it. The quiet forest had become a beehive of activity, but I felt detached—as if my mind were still stuck at the moment before I found the body, when I had been peacefully walking along the path.

I looked up into the eyes of a young man with strawberry-blond hair and blue eyes. He held my wrist in his hand, taking my pulse, and I absently wondered if he played piano, because he had such long, slim fingers. I asked him shakily, "Do you know who that is?"

He shook his head. "Sorry, I don't know." His voice was low and soothing. "How are you feeling?"

"I'm okay now," I answered. "It was just the shock. I'd been talking to her, trying to reassure her, thinking she was just hurt, and all the while, she was already dead!" I started to cry.

He stood awkwardly by my side, as if he wasn't sure what to do with a crying middle-aged woman who had just fainted. I pulled myself together and gave him a watery smile to try to reassure him that I was done falling apart. He reached down, removed the blood pressure cuff, and then helped me to my feet.

"Thanks," I said as I stood unsteadily. The world spun for a moment before settling back into focus.

About this time, a tall, broad-shouldered man in a police uniform, who looked like he might have played football when he was younger, walked up and asked him, "Okay to ask her some questions?"

The EMT nodded and headed back up the trail as I turned to face the officer.

"What's your name?" he asked.

"I'm Ellen Douglas," I replied, reaching out to shake his hand. His hand felt warm to my freezing palm.

"James Andrews, Chief of Police," he introduced himself. He appeared to be about my age or a bit older. It was hard to tell. He had dark hair with some gray peaking through and perceptive blue eyes. His whole demeanor spoke of quiet competence.

I felt myself relax a bit. "I'd say it's nice to meet you, but it really isn't, under these circumstances," I responded as he ushered me a little way back along the trail to where there was a bench we could sit on. "I do enjoy your posts on the town Facebook page."

"Thanks! I try to be as helpful as I can. You're Noelle's Mom, aren't you?" he asked as we sat down. I nodded. "I'm surprised I haven't met you before," he continued.

"Me too, although your face does look familiar, so we've probably seen each other, just not been introduced."

"You look familiar to me, too. Do you walk here often?" he asked.

"A few times a week in the mornings since I retired. Before that, I came occasionally after work when Louisa and I needed some fresh air." I began to relax the more we talked, which was probably why he was easing into the conversation.

"What did you do before you retired?" he asked.

"I was a child labor investigator for the Federal Government for over 30 years," I said proudly. "Retirement is a big adjustment, and with Noelle moving to Indianapolis to be closer to school, it's been a lot of changes in a short period of time."

"I'm sure it has. I imagine being a Child Labor investigator would make you pretty observant, so can you tell me what happened today?" He paused and then added, "Be as specific as you can."

I felt my heart pounding inside my chest as I thought about finding the woman's body. I took a deep breath and let it out slowly to calm myself. I was still horrified by what I had seen and didn't really want to relive it. "I was out here walking my dog." I gestured to Louisa, who started wagging her tail at the attention.

He briefly smiled and then gestured with his hand for me to continue.

"We'd stopped so I could give her some water..." I trailed off as I realized I no longer knew where her water bowl and my bottle were. I shook my head, realizing that wasn't important right now. I could ask him once I'd explained. "I saw the tree branch across the path and approached to see if we could get around it and continue on to the falls, or if we would have to turn back. Suddenly, Louisa pulled loose from me and jumped over the branch. When I went after her, I saw a ponytail and a woman's leg, but I couldn't figure out how to get to her without potentially hurting her more. Except I guess I couldn't have hurt her, could I?" Tears welled up in my eyes again as I looked at the police chief. My throat felt tight, and I hugged my arms around myself as if doing so would keep me from falling apart.

"You couldn't have known that," he said kindly and patted my arm. I appreciated his comfort so much, as I was still reeling. "So, then you called 9-1-1?"

"Yes."

"Did you hear anything before you got to this point on the trail?"

"Hear anything?" I asked, puzzled. "Oh, do you mean did I hear the sound of the limb falling? I didn't hear anything like that. There were lots of other noises in the woods, and my dog likes to bark at all the squirrels, so it would have to be really loud for me to have heard it," I explained. "It was odd, though, about the limb. I didn't think that part of the forest got damaged in the tornado, so I was surprised to see the limb had fallen there."

He nodded. "Did you see any other people on the trails?"

"Not today. I normally pass at least a few other people while we're out here, but I got a later start today, so I'm guessing the people I normally see would have already gone through." I shrugged.

"Do you know any of them by name?" he asked.

"No," I said slowly, thinking about who I had seen. "I have exchanged greetings with them before, but we haven't introduced ourselves. They are mostly older couples or young moms out with their preschoolers."

"That's OK. Where did you park?" he asked.

"In the parking lot over by the shelter house," I answered.

"Were there a lot of other cars there?"

I nodded. There were always lots of cars in the park.

"Do you remember any in particular?"

"Hmm…" I paused to think, wondering what that had to do with the accident, unless they were trying to find the victim's car. "There was a Tesla. It was one of the ones that had doors that opened like a DeLorean. Pretty fancy for around here, so it caught my eye. There were also a couple of trucks and some SUVs. Maybe a BMW. I do remember thinking I wasn't sure I was allowed to park there since everyone else's cars were black."

The edges of his mouth tipped up at that.

"My car is blackberry, so I guess it was close enough," I continued, hoping to make him smile again. His eyes softened when he smiled, and it made me feel safe.

"Well, thank you for speaking with me. Can I get your information in case I have any other questions?" he asked.

He handed me a small notebook, and I wrote down my name, address, and phone number. As he started to walk away, I reached out and touched his hand.

"Can you tell me who it was?" I asked tentatively, afraid of the answer. "She seemed familiar."

"I'm sorry," he said. "We haven't notified her next of kin yet, so I can't tell you anything."

I nodded in understanding.

He started to turn away and then stopped. "Would you like a lift back to your car? I can have one of my officers take you to the other parking lot."

"I would really appreciate that," I said in acceptance since I was still feeling a bit woozy after fainting.

He waved over another officer, and I took hold of Louisa's leash more firmly and followed the officer to her car. All I wanted to do now was go home and call my mom and my daughter, just to let them know I loved them. Life seemed very uncertain at this moment, and I wanted to make sure they knew how I felt.

Chapter Three

The next morning, my alarm went off at eight, but I'd barely had any sleep. I'd been tossing and turning all night. I kept seeing the woman's sightless eyes staring up at me. Late last night, I found out on Facebook that the victim was someone I knew, Natalie Boule. No wonder she'd looked familiar. Natalie owned Someone Else's Closet, a clothing rental and consignment shop in Cascade. I shopped there every few months when I lost a little weight or put a little on, and I needed a few articles of clothing to tide me over until I could fit back into my regular clothes. I hadn't been into the shop for a while because I was trying to wait until I'd lost a few more pounds and could reward myself with clothes at least two sizes down from what I'd been wearing.

Natalie was young—thirty or thirty-one, if I remembered correctly. She was an attractive blonde with a bubbly personality who was always perfectly dressed for any occasion. Everyone really liked her. I couldn't believe she had been hit by a tree while running in the park. It just felt so senseless. She had so much to live for, and then to be struck down in such a freak accident? I was heartbroken, and I didn't even know her that well. I couldn't imagine how her family and close friends were feeling. I also had that weird feeling you get when you think, *"That could have been me if..."*

I dragged myself out of bed, threw on some jeans and a T-shirt, and decided I was too depressed to stay home alone. I pulled my shoulder-length brown hair into a pony-tail and headed for Frankie's Diner. I needed comfort food and people. Frankie's was an old-fashioned small-town din-er with red vinyl booths along the walls and a scattering of tables throughout the center of the room. On one side was an L-shaped counter with stools wrapped around it. Frankie was a bit younger than me and presided over the restaurant with a strong personality and a sense of humor. She often played practical jokes on her customers and could dish it right back to anyone who teased her. There were pithy sayings on the walls, and the specials board normally had a saying for the day. In one corner close to the counter was the pie cabinet, which was filled with all kinds of yummy pies. I ate there at least a couple of times a week. Frankie's husband and her two daughters all worked at the diner, and I had become friends with their whole family.

When I walked in, I was engulfed in the familiar smells of bacon, toast, and coffee. I slid onto the stool at the end—my favorite—as Kristi and Maria, the waitresses, greeted me. "Diet Dr. Pepper, right?" Kristi asked before setting it in front of me. She was short like me but had a huge personality that had her joking, singing, and generally being the life of the party at the diner.

Normally, I greeted her enthusiastically, but I didn't have it in me this morning. I gave her a little half smile.

"What's wrong?" she asked, pausing her normal rushing around to really look at me.

"Did you hear about the accident in the park yesterday?" I asked.

She nodded, her eyes getting big.

"Well, I'm the one who found her," I said and blinked back more tears. "I'm really shaken up."

"Oh, honey!" she said. "You need comfort food! Do you want some pie?" She knew it was my weakness.

"I think I want some biscuits and gravy this morning," I said and then added, "But maybe pie after." My stomach growled, and I realized that despite feeling down, I was really hungry.

"How did you find her?" Kristi asked, and I told her about walking Louisa in the park and finding the body. Everyone at the counter was listening, and I noticed a particularly attractive man at the other end who seemed to be busily working at his computer but glanced up at me while I told my story. He was tall and appeared to be younger than me, although he had a bit of gray showing at the temples of his dark hair. I was pretty sure I'd never seen him here before. I'd have to ask Kristi about him if he left before I did.

As I was answering Kristi's questions, I saw Frankie—a plump woman with curly brown hair, dressed in jeans and a black shirt with a pumpkin on it—coming out of the kitchen. I paused in my story to greet her, but just as I started to say hello, her cell phone rang. She held up a finger to tell me just a minute, and I watched as her face paled.

"Oh no," she said. "Why do they think that? What are you going to do?" She paused for a minute to listen and then began rattling off more questions. "What did you tell them? Do I need to hire a lawyer?" She barely gave the person on the other end a chance to respond. She hung up the phone, came over, and leaned on the end of the counter with a worried expression on her face.

"What's wrong?" I asked.

"That was my brother, Tony. He said the police were just there asking him questions about Natalie's death."

"Why would they do that?" I asked, puzzled. "She died in an accident. I ought to know. I'm the one who found her."

"Apparently," she replied, "the tree isn't what killed her. The police think it was placed on her body to make it look like an accident."

Stunned, I sat there for a moment as the other people around the counter gasped and gossiped over this news. She was murdered! I'd found a murder victim! Was the killer still there when I found her? Had I just missed seeing them? Would the police suspect me?

The clinking of silverware against plates finally brought my focus back to the conversation, and I heard Frankie saying that she was very worried about her brother. "But why would the police suspect him?" I asked.

Frankie shook her head at me. "Didn't you know they dated for several years? I thought one day she would be my sister-in-law, but Tony wasn't ready to commit, and she was ready to settle down, so she broke up with him and moved on about a year ago. She had just gotten engaged to Max Holland, a lawyer from Indianapolis, a couple of months ago."

Frankie teared up, and I hopped off my stool to give her a hug.

"This must be just awful for you!" I exclaimed as I hugged her. "Is there anything I can do to help?"

"Unless you know how to clear my brother's name, I don't see how," she said. "But it's sweet of you to offer. Now, who needs coffee?" She pulled herself together and started through the room with coffeepots in hand.

"Poor Frankie!" I said more to myself than to the group.

To my surprise, the attractive man I had noticed earlier interjected. "You aren't really going to try to clear her brother's name, are you? With all due respect, I think a murder investigation is a bit more complex than a bake sale."

I immediately felt like I'd been challenged. Did he think I wasn't smart enough to figure this out? I may be a middle-aged, full-figured, small-town girl, but I've read thousands of mystery books. Surely, I could help figure this one out. I hated being dismissed or underestimated, and sometimes I acted rashly when I felt that way. I needed to not let his condescension egg me into doing something I didn't want to do.

I looked at him and said in a very flat tone of voice, "You never know."

He blinked back at me, surprised, but I turned to my food and let the conversation of the other people at the diner roll over me as I finished my breakfast and contemplated what it would take to clear someone's name in a murder case. I knew Frankie hadn't been serious about me clearing Tony's name, but I felt some responsibility to Natalie since I was the one who found her. I had been a child labor investigator for thirty years, and I was very good at talking to people. I was sure that, between my eye for detail and the fact that people naturally confided in me, I could find a way to help. It couldn't hurt to ask a few questions around town, even if that was all I did. But as I paid the bill, I thought that maybe whoever did this wouldn't be very happy about me asking questions. I would need to be discreet if I were going to ask around about the murder.

— ❧ —

Chapter Four

After polishing off a piece of cherry pie and bidding farewell to Frankie and Kristi, I headed for my favorite home away from home, the coffee shop. The Grounds, a converted Victorian house, was in a perfect spot midway between Main Street and the park. The outside was yellow, with accents in shades of purple and violet. The inside had cozy chairs and couches in conversation groups with a few tables scattered around. The bell dinged as I opened the door, and Noelle looked up and smiled.

"Hi, Mom!" She came around the counter and hugged me.

My nineteen-year-old daughter was short and curvy with a mass of curly black hair. She was wearing the customary uniform for the coffee shop— jeans and a black "The Grounds" T-shirt.

"How are you holding up?" she asked as she slipped around the counter and pulled down my ceramic mug. It had a big red heart on the side. She'd made it for me several years ago at one of the places where you painted your own pottery.

It stayed here at The Grounds since I most often drank hot drinks here.

As she began making my usual raspberry hot chocolate, I replied, "I'm still shaken up, especially after finding out it was Natalie. Had you heard that?"

She nodded. "I also heard that the tree might not have been what killed her."

I shook my head. "I just can't believe that someone would want to hurt her. She was always so sweet to everyone."

"I know." She handed me my mug and tilted her head toward the scones.

I shook my head since I'd just had pie.

"She was in here a lot since her shop is so close, and she always seemed to be upbeat. She knew everyone and would chat with whoever she was in line with while she waited to order. Natalie was good to us baristas, too. She gave generous tips, and at Christmas, she gave us all stuff from her store, like scarves, gloves, and purses. I really liked her!"

"I did too. I loved going into her shop, and she was always so helpful when I didn't know what to get." I sighed and went to sit down somewhere comfy. I was appreciating the familiar today, as yesterday had been way outside my comfort zone.

Since it was slow in the coffee shop, Noelle joined me on the couch by the fireplace. "I've been hearing a lot of strange theories this morning about who might have killed her. It's all anyone has talked about. People are saying it was her ex-boyfriend, her partner, or her current fiancé. I even heard someone say it was probably you since you found the body."

She began to laugh as I stared at her in shock. "I'm sure they just said that to give me a hard time because I was out of their sugar-free caramel syrup," she said. "They know better."

"So, what specifically did you hear about the 'actual' suspects?" I asked, making air quotes.

"People are saying something was going on between Natalie and her ex behind Max's back, but they seem split between whether Natalie was breaking up with Max to get back with her ex or if that was just what her ex wanted. Then they blame Tara because she will likely inherit the business, so they think she has a financial motive. I can't really see that, as she and Natalie have always been so close." She narrowed her eyes. "Why do you care what people are saying?" she asked.

"Well, I feel sort of a sense of responsibility since I found her. And then at Frankie's just now, I found out Natalie's ex is Frankie's brother, Tony."

"Mother, please tell me you are just curious and not about to do something stupid, like trying to investigate." Noelle frowned, and her eyebrows scrunched together. "This is a murder, not some employer working kids too late on a school night."

"I know it's a murder, and I'm not investigating...exactly," I replied. "I just thought if I talked to some people, I could maybe help clear his name, but it sounds like I might need to clear my own too," I said, still in shock that someone would think I could have done something so horrible.

"I don't think anyone seriously suspects you," she said, quick to reassure me. "They just said something like the person to find the body is always a suspect. I think they've just read too many mysteries, like someone else I know." She gave me a stern look.

"Now, Mother," she began to lecture, but then the bell dinged, and who should come striding into the coffee shop but the stranger from Frankie's. Noelle leaned down and hissed, "This discussion is not over."

I rolled my eyes as she walked over to the counter. Which one of us was the mom, anyway?

I focused on the conversation Noelle was having with Mr. Tall, Dark, and Handsome. "What name should I call when I have it ready?" she asked.

"Tom," he mumbled, not really paying attention as he looked at his phone.

Whatever he was looking at had him completely engrossed, so he almost didn't respond when my daughter asked, "Is this your first time at The Grounds?"

He looked up and smiled. I felt warmth all the way to my toes. He may not have thought much of my investigating, but he had a killer smile. I was a little unsettled by my reaction to him. "Yes. I'm thinking of moving here from out of state. It seems like my kind of place. You'll probably see a lot of me."

She smiled back at him and rang up his coffee on the register. "I'm only here part-time, since I'm in school," she said, "but I'm sure we'll run into each other again. It's not like this is a budding metropolis." She laughed and then turned away to make his latte.

He turned around and jerked to a stop when he saw me. I decided that rather than have another unpleasant conversation with him or another lecture from my daughter, now would be a very good time to make myself scarce. I brushed by him and would have ignored him completely, but he reached out and touched my arm.

"I hope you weren't offended by what I said at the diner," he said contritely.

I looked at his hand on my arm, and he quickly let go. "I appreciate the apology," I said stiffly and moved past him. I waved goodbye to my daughter. "Talk to you later, Noelle!" I said as I hurried out. I glanced back to find they were both staring after me with nearly identical frowns.

Chapter Five

I decided I wasn't really ready to go home yet, so I turned toward downtown. I noticed there was a Tesla parked in front of The Grounds. There'd been one at Frankie's too, so I bet it belonged to Tom. That was interesting. It looked like the one I saw at the park before I went on my walk. I bet Tom was there yesterday. Our little town didn't have very many Teslas, so it seemed really likely. I wondered if he'd seen anything. I might have to try to find that out.

As I continued walking toward downtown, I found myself feeling a bit cranky. Why did my daughter think it was so absurd for me to want to ask some questions about a murder victim I found? I was a trained investigator. I realized child labor wasn't the same thing as a murder investigation, but I did know how to interview people and look for evidence. Besides, being curious was what made me so good at my job for so many years. Just because I had retired from it didn't mean I didn't still have what it took to figure out what happened to Natalie. And in a way, I felt responsible since I found her.

I really didn't consciously head there, but I shortly found myself staring at the wooden sign printed with an elaborate script font that said *Someone Else's Closet*. It was a narrow storefront nestled between an art studio and an antique store right in the middle of the business district downtown. In the window was a mannequin dressed in a red tunic-length sweater with black and white herringbone-patterned leggings and black booties. Natalie was known for putting together cool outfits in her window that drew people in, and I was sure this was one of hers. It made me sad to think that it was the last one she would ever do. Inside, the lights were out, but through the window I could see the exposed bricks on one side and the long, narrow room filled with racks of clothes. About three-quarters of the way back was the desk area, with dressing rooms and accessories at the back.

Just as I was about to walk away from the store, I noticed movement. I realized Natalie's partner, Tara, was walking toward the door. I pulled back as she opened the door, but she still jumped when she turned around from turning the lock.

"I'm so sorry, Tara! I didn't mean to startle you. I was just looking at the beautiful outfit in the window," I said. "I didn't really expect anyone to be here today."

"That's okay." She turned to look at the display. "It is a great ensemble, isn't it?" she said with a wan smile. "Natalie did it yesterday morning. She was always so good at putting together outfits that popped. That's never been my forte, so I'm not sure what I'll do now."

Tara Grace was a tall, dark-haired woman in her mid-thirties whose normally perfectly quaffed brunette bob was di sheveled, and her green eyes were red-rimmed and swollen. She had clearly been crying for some time.

"Oh, Tara, I can't even imagine how you feel today." I gave her a brief side-hug. "What are you doing here, anyway? Surely no one would expect you to open the shop today."

"I didn't really want to come in, but I had a delivery coming and no one else to be here to receive it." She sniffled. "I really do just want to be home, but now it's just me," she said as tears threatened to fall from her brimming eyes.

"I know how close you were," I said sympathetically.

"We'd been best friends our whole lives. That's just it," she said. "The last time I spoke with her, we argued, and now I'll never get the chance to say I'm sorry!" She wailed as the tears poured down her face.

I handed her a tissue and patted her arm. "I'm sure she knew you still cared about her. I've never seen you two fight before."

"We didn't normally," she replied. "But she'd been acting so secretively the last few days and had been really irritable. I thought it was because her fiancé wasn't treating her right, and I made the mistake of saying that. I should have kept my mouth shut!" she exclaimed. "She didn't want to talk about what was wrong. She told me to mind my own business and stormed out. I hate that the last things we said to each other were said in anger."

"You'd been friends for a long time, so I'm sure the next time you saw her, everything would have been okay," I said reassuringly. "Is there anything I can do to help?"

She shook her head. "I'm just going to head home for now. I have to meet Natalie's family in a little while at the funeral home to help plan the arrangements."

I waved as she turned toward her car.

Poor Tara, I thought. It would be awful to have a fight with your best friend and then never get to make up before she died. But then another thought came to me. What if their argument was more serious than Tara was letting on? And what did she mean about Natalie's fiancé not treating her right? So much for asking the right questions. I'd just had the perfect opportunity to find out more, and I'd blown it. Maybe my skills had slipped. I shook my head in frustration. I needed to make a list.

I speed-walked the two blocks back to my car, grabbed a notebook I kept in the glove compartment, and started jotting down the questions I had:

1. Did Natalie go jogging to blow off some steam after the argument with Tara?

2. What did Tara mean about Natalie's fiancé not treating her right? Was he abusive?

3. Why did the police suspect Frankie's brother, Tony, over her current fiancé?

I know the boyfriend is always a suspect, but is there something else that makes them suspect him?.

1. If the tree didn't kill Natalie, what did kill her?

2. What exactly did Noelle hear from people about Tara, Tony, and Natalie's fiancé, Max? Did she tell me

everything she'd heard?

I wasn't sure since the new guy interrupted our conversation.

I decided that was a good start. Now I just had to figure out how to get the answers to those questions. I mused about how to go about it as I started my car toward home. When I first started as a child labor investigator, I often had people confess violations to me because they underestimated me. They thought they were "explaining" to a young girl how the business world worked. The shocked look on their faces when I handed them a notice of findings almost made me laugh. But they couldn't dispute anything because they themselves had admitted to the violations in their own words.

As I got older, my natural friendliness led people to confide in me. Depending on their age, they either treated me like their mom or their sister, and they still "explained" to me why what they were doing wasn't really a problem. It always amazed me how much people would reveal, even knowing from the start that I was an investigator for the U.S. government. It was almost like they forgot who I worked for once they started talking to me.

In the case of Natalie's death, I wasn't planning on announcing that I was looking into her murder, but I was hoping that people would still find me approachable, which might lead them to reveal more than they intended.

I needed to let Lou out and take her for a walk while I thought about who I should talk to next.

Chapter Six

took Louisa out to another park in a nearby town since I couldn't face the Cascade Falls trails again yet. This park was farther from home, but Louisa loved walking here and set a blistering pace. The path was wider and partly paved, but the foliage was less dense, and in many places you could see the houses built just outside the park through it. There was the scent of woodsmoke coming from the campground, and traffic sounds from the nearby road.

There were even more squirrels than at Cascade Falls, and at the beginning of our walk, I had to focus on keeping Louisa from yanking the leash off my wrist and taking off after them. Once she had settled down a bit, my mind began replaying the details of the murder, but I wasn't getting anywhere. I had too many questions and not nearly enough information to figure out any answers, and I wasn't sure who I could safely ask. After all, if I asked the wrong person, it could be dangerous.

I was almost relieved when my phone rang. It was my daughter calling to continue the conversation we'd started at the coffee shop.

"Mother, just to be clear, it is a terrible idea for you to be asking questions about a murder!" Noelle said forcefully.

"Hey, did that guy Tom stay in the shop for long?" I asked, quickly changing the subject so I didn't have to answer her. "He was at Frankie's while I was eating breakfast and seemed pretty arrogant."

"Don't think I don't know you are changing the subject, Mother."

I hated it when she called me "Mother" in that tone, like I was a child she had to look after.

"He stayed a couple of hours working on his computer. We chatted a bit. I think he seems really nice. He was funny too. He had all of us behind the counter in stitches."

"Really?" I said, surprised.

"He asked about you, too," she said. "I think he might be attracted to you, Mom."

That was more like it. I was back to being Mom instead of Mother.

"So, what do you think?" she asked, but I had clearly missed something while I was thinking.

"About..." I asked.

"Going out with Tom. Weren't you listening? I said he asked about you. I bet if you come in tomorrow to The Grounds, he'll be there again." She sounded almost pleading.

"Since when are you so interested in my love life?" I chuckled, and she growled on the other end of the line. "I don't know that I'm interested in going out with anyone, honey,"

I said, shaking my head as I walked. I hadn't had a serious relationship in years. My life was full of taking care of my mom and my daughter.

"But I thought you were ready to explore those roads you didn't take when you were younger," she said. "Maybe a man to do things with is one of those roads you should explore. I'm not saying you have to marry him. Just get to know him better. I don't want you to be lonely. If you're worried about me or how I'm going to react, don't be! I want you to be happy, and if being in a relationship would make you happy, then that's what I want for you. I think Dad would have wanted that too."

My daughter certainly could be persuasive when she wanted to and had hit on almost all the things I'd been saying to myself. "I'll think about it, honey."

She had to go, so we exchanged "I love yous" and hung up, leaving me with lots to think about.

Did I want to explore a relationship or even just a friend-ship with a man? I had loved my husband with my whole heart. We met in college on a bus to Florida for spring break with the campus ministry we both attended. I had seen him before, but we'd never talked until the trip down to Florida, when the group he was with needed a fourth for Euchre. He and I were partners, and after we won three games in a row, we moved to another seat and talked for the rest of the journey. Besides loving to play cards, both of us were on the worship team at our respective churches. For the rest of the trip, we were inseparable. And that shared attraction grew throughout the week. We had only been home for a couple of hours when he called to ask me out for dinner.

The first summer after we started dating, we both went home to our hometowns, but we talked on the phone every day and visited each other whenever we could. Both families were welcoming, but he was not as close to his family as I was to mine. At the end of the summer, he proposed in the little gazebo in Cascade Falls Park, and we got married right after graduation. We were head over heels for each other and settled into a life where we both felt incomplete without the other. I could count on one hand the number of nights we spent apart in our entire marriage. Our love just expanded when our little girl came along.

Then, ten years ago, we were on vacation with Noelle in Tennessee. My hearty husband, who was never sick a day in his life, suddenly started having digestive problems and felt so bad, we cut our trip short and went home. The first doctor he saw said it was the flu, and he should rest, but when he was no better after a week, we sought a second opinion. They admitted him to the hospital and started running tests. Liver cancer, they told me, but it was already too late by the time we had the diagnosis. A few days later, he was gone. My soul mate was gone.

I was lost. I didn't know how to do life without him, but I couldn't just curl up in a ball and quit living like I wanted to. I had a ten-year-old daughter who was trying so hard to be strong for me that she wouldn't allow herself to grieve. Finally, six months after his death, she broke down, and I dragged myself up from the pit I had been wallowing in, and we both began to try to find a new normal.

I really hadn't had any interest in dating while I raised Noelle for the last ten years. We were both so devastated by the loss of my husband—her father—that we just clung to each other and made our own little bubble with just us and my mom.

Lately, since she had moved out to be closer to school, I'd been pretty lonely. But I didn't want her to feel like she had to organize her life around mine. She needed to be hanging out with friends her own age. I didn't want to hold her back or have her worried about me. But was I really ready? The thought of dating again wasn't enticing. In fact, just the idea of going on a date made my heart race. I wasn't sure if I would even know how to act on a date after being married and then a widow for so long.

And if I did want to explore something, was Tom really the right person? He was attractive, and when I'd first seen him at the diner, I'd felt something stir within me that I hadn't felt since my husband. But good looks and a killer smile weren't everything, and I felt like he'd been condescending at Frankie's. I hated being condescended to. It was my number one pet peeve. I would give it some thought. I didn't have to decide right now. It might be a moot point, since I doubted I would see him again anyway.

Louisa pulled on her leash, impatient with my woolgathering, and I picked up the pace to keep up with her. I shook off thoughts of my love life, or lack thereof, and refocused on something I might actually make sense of. Noelle's matchmaking had distracted me, and I'd forgotten to ask her if she had heard anything else about the murder. She might not tell me, of course, since she didn't want me to ask questions, but as a mother, I was good at getting her to tell me things she didn't intend to, so I was pretty sure I could pry it out of her.

I reached for my water bottle and realized I had also for-gotten to ask the police chief about my collapsible bowl. I was going to need to go down to the police station and see if they had it. Maybe I could do that tomorrow morning. I felt like I was forgetting something else. It was right on the edge of my brain, but I couldn't pull it to the forefront.

Oh, well. Maybe if I stopped trying, it would come to me.

Chapter Seven

When I awoke the next morning, I realized what I had forgotten. The paper! The one in Louisa's mouth. What if it was a clue? I jumped out of bed and rushed to the hamper to find the sweatshirt I'd been wearing. I pulled out the paper and quickly saw that it was part of a note. It was from a small, lined steno pad, the kind I had used almost every day of my career to keep notes. It appeared the paper had been torn in half, and it didn't help that Louisa had chewed on it. It was no longer damp from Louisa's mouth, but it had that brittle texture paper got after it dried. It was hard to make out, but I could see the words *warning*, *meet*, and *park*, along with the number *10*. Maybe Natalie hadn't been in the park for a run after all. Maybe she was there to meet someone. And what did the "warning" mean? I felt a sinking sensation in my stomach at the thought that Natalie might have known she was in danger. Was someone threatening her? Or were they warning her about someone or something else? But who? And why meet in the park when there were restaurants, coffee shops, and even her business that would have been more convenient? Clearly, this piece of paper caused more questions than it answered.

And the bigger problem was I didn't know where exactly Louisa had picked it up. The timing would have been right to be from Natalie, but it also could have been lying on the ground for a while. Well, probably not too long, or it would have been covered in mud or dirt, but it didn't have to be Natalie's. I looked at Louisa. "I sure wish you could talk and tell me where you found this."

But what should I do with it? I didn't know if it was important or not. And that was the problem. If it *was* important, I could be accused of withholding evidence in a crime, but if it wasn't important, they might think I was some crazy conspiracy theorist or something.

My gut told me it was important, and my gut normally didn't steer me wrong. I thought I'd better err on the side of caution and take this to the police.

I guess I need to go to the police station for more than just asking about Louisa's bowl, I thought as I hurriedly pulled on some jeans and a pullover sweater. This could be important.

I fed Louisa and let her out before heading toward town. My house was a one-story ranch-style home set about 100 yards back from the road. My front yard was enormous with lots of mature trees, but I still had enough of a backyard to give Louisa room to run inside the fence. As I was pulling out of my driveway, I had the funny feeling that someone was watching me, but I shrugged it off. I was probably just still spooked from finding the body.

I pulled up outside the town's police station. It really was more of a storefront, with the front covered in windows. The door opened into a large room with a counter and several desks scattered about. A short hall appeared to lead back to some private offices. It had a slight musty smell, like someone had let wet clothes sit for too long before drying them.

As I made my way to the counter, I saw the chief of police standing at the entrance to the hallway talking to another man, whose back was to me. He was tall and looked somewhat familiar, but I couldn't see him well enough to identify him.

"Can I help you?" A woman's voice drew my attention back to the counter. "Oh! Hi, Ellen!" she went on. She was a little taller than me with short dark curls and a soft, curvy build that spoke more of strength than softness. She didn't show her age at all, and I realized it was someone I'd graduated from high school with.

"Hi, Becky!" I replied. "I didn't realize you were working here now. I thought you were still at the fire station."

"I am." She smiled. "I just help out here occasionally when they need it. The normal receptionist is out on maternity leave, so I'm filling in for the next few weeks when I'm not on shift at the fire station. How have you been?"

"Pretty good. I just took early retirement from my job, so I'm figuring out what to do with myself."

"Must be nice," she said, but there was no bite to it. "What brings you in here?"

"Well," I said as I tried to figure out how to begin, but before I could get anything else out, I heard the chief say, "Mrs. Douglas, I'm glad you stopped by. I needed to talk to you."

He reached out to shake hands with the man he had been speaking with and said, "I'll be in touch as soon as I have more information." As the man turned to leave, I felt a little frisson of awareness when I saw it was the mystery man, Tom. I'm sure my face must have given away my shock, because he smirked as he nodded hello to me and quickly left.

"Right this way, Mrs. Douglas." The chief ushered me down the hall to a private office. It wasn't large but had a window overlooking the parking lot and the street beyond, a wooden desk with two fairly uncomfortable-looking wooden chairs in front of it, and several metal filing cabinets.

"Please call me Ellen," I said as I perched on one of the chairs. Suddenly, my palms grew clammy. I was nervous about being here, and I had no idea why.

"Ellen, I would like you to sign a statement with the information you gave us the other day," he said. "I was just about to call you to ask you to come in."

"Oh," I said, a little surprised. "Sure. I'd be happy to."

"What brought you in today?" he asked as he sat behind his desk and pulled out a paper, which I assumed was the statement he wanted me to sign.

"Well, I remembered something I'd forgotten all about when I spoke to you before." I pulled out the slip of paper and handed it across the desk before continuing. "I pulled this out of Louisa's mouth shortly after we found Natalie. I stuck it in my pocket and forgot all about it until this morning. Do you think she could have been meeting someone out in the park?" I asked eagerly.

"Now, Ellen," he said, shaking his head, "I'm not going to speculate about an open investigation with you, but thank you for bringing this in. We'll have to see what we can glean from it, but having been in your dog's mouth, it probably isn't going to tell us much now." He frowned. "Anything else you've remembered?" he asked, piercing me with his blue eyes.

"Noooo," I said hesitantly. "But I did wonder if you knew that Natalie and her business partner had a huge argument the morning she died."

"And how do you know about that?" he asked, raising his eyebrows at me.

"I ran into Tara outside her shop, and she told me about it," I replied.

"Just happened to run into her, or did you seek her out to try to dig up information?" he asked with iron in his tone.

"I—" I started to reply, but he held up his hand.

"I don't want to know, but let's get something straight here," he said gruffly. "Ellen, this is a murder investigation. There is a killer on the loose, and you need to keep your head down." He stared right into my eyes as he said the last part, and I shuddered.

"Okay," I squeaked out, thoroughly intimidated. "I'll leave the investigating to you." My voice was a little shaky as I said it...and at the time, I meant it.

Chapter Eight

I read and signed my statement and left the police station. I was shaken and felt the need for a little comfort, so I headed to the retirement home to visit my mother. My mom was ninety but looked like she was in her seventies. She was a petite, white-haired dynamo who was always dressed impeccably. Today was no exception. She had on a lavender sweater set with gray slacks. A long strand of pearls was looped multiple times around her neck. Her only concession to aging was the flat black shoes she was wearing instead of the heels she always wore when I was young. In the last year or so, she had started needing a cane to help her keep her balance, but she made sure her cane was her favorite color, purple. Even with the cane, she was still the spryest ninety-year-old I'd ever seen. I sure hoped I had inherited those genes.

I found her in the activity room playing bingo. I hated to interrupt her, since I knew she really loved playing it and won prizes almost every time. I was going to leave and come back later, but she spied me in the doorway and insisted on coming back to her room with me. She had a two-room apartment with a small kitchen and attached living room on one side and her bedroom and bathroom through a doorway on the other. She had it decorated with all kinds of pottery she had collected over the years from her various vacations. She used to collect cookbooks when she traveled, too, but she no longer cooked after she moved into the retirement home. We'd given them out to various family members to enjoy. I'd kept some of my favorites and sometimes brought her baked goods I'd made using her recipes.

Her living room held a couch in front of the window and two recliners facing a TV. She sat in her favorite recliner and motioned me to the other chair. All she wanted to talk about was the murder. She immediately started grilling me about finding the body. I told her everything I'd learned and finished with the warning the chief had given me to stay out of it.

"Oh, don't worry about that," she said dismissively, waving her hand in the air. "But why is it that you feel like you have to investigate this?"

I sat silently for a moment, considering. "I think it's several things. I feel responsible somehow since I found Natalie. And I want to help clear Frankie's brother's name. And to be honest, I've been feeling at loose ends since I retired, and that may be part of it, too. I'm a really good investigator. And that's been such an integral part of my life for so long, it just seems natural to use those skills to try to figure out what happened."

She nodded as I made each point. "In that case, I have lots of information you need to know."

"How do you have information?" I asked, mystified. I knew the retirement home was a hotbed of gossip from the many things Mom had told me since she moved in, but surely, they couldn't really have clues to a murder, could they?

"Frankie's aunt Anita ate lunch at my table," she said. "She was really upset because the police had brought Tony in for questioning."

"I thought they had already questioned him at home the day after the murder," I said, remembering the conversation with Frankie at the diner.

"Apparently, they had more questions, and this time they made him go to the police station. He's been there for hours, from what Anita said."

"Oh dear! For Frankie's sake, I hope he didn't do it."

My mother nodded in agreement.

"Did Aunt Anita tell you anything else?"

She answered eagerly. "She told me all about Tony and Natalie's relationship. I guess they were madly in love. They dated for about five years, and Natalie was ready to settle down, get married, and have a family. Tony wasn't sure he was ready for that, so Natalie broke it off."

That was what Frankie had told me, too. "So, Aunt Anita knew Natalie?"

"Yes, and she really liked her. That's why she was so excited when she found out that Tony had started having second thoughts about letting Natalie go. I guess once Tony found out she was engaged to someone else, it made him realize what he had given up."

"She was a wonderful person, so I can understand wanting to be with her."

She nodded. "And sometimes it takes a little jealousy for a man to realize what he has been taking for granted. That's how I got your father to ask me to marry him, you know."

I did know, but I loved hearing the story anyway, so I just smiled as she went on.

"I told him I was going to move to Florida in three weeks, and he proposed the next day, and instead of being in Florida, I was married in three weeks." She smiled nostalgically.

"Do you know how he let her know he wanted her back?" I asked, deciding I'd better bring us back to the topic at hand.

"According to Anita, in the last few months, he had started leaving her little presents and sending her messages telling her he missed her and wanted her back."

"Did his aunt know how Natalie responded to Tony's pursuit?" I asked, wondering if this was why the police suspected Tony. A spurned lover would make a good suspect.

"She said that at first Natalie wouldn't give him the time of day and kept returning the gifts, but all that changed a couple of weeks ago," she answered. "Anita said Tony told her that he really thought maybe Natalie was willing to give him another chance. They had dinner the night before she was killed—at a restaurant a few miles away, so no one saw them together—and she told Tony she was going to break off her engagement."

"Did she tell him what happened to change her mind?" I asked.

"If she did, Anita didn't know it," she said, "and since no one else heard what was said that night, the police have accused Tony of being the one she rejected, which would give him a motive for murder."

She sat back in her chair, clearly worn out. I supposed gossiping could be exhausting. We talked about other things for a few minutes before I hugged her and told her I'd talk to her in a few days. She assured me she'd let me know if she heard anything else.

As I walked out to my car, I couldn't help but think that my mom in the retirement home had gathered way more information than I had. Maybe she should be the one investigating this murder! I wondered what else she might find out from her friends. And what about my friends? Might any of them be able to shed light on what happened to Natalie? I really needed to sit down and think about who I knew that might know something. So far, I had just stumbled upon every piece of information I had. If I really wanted to know what happened, I needed to find a way to be more focused on trying to get answers to the questions I had come up with.

I was planning to go home and sit down with a pad and paper and do a little brainstorming. But when I got to my car, I found all four of my tires flat and red paint dripping down the back window from the words, *Stop asking questions!* For the second time in two days, I felt the breath freeze in my body, and I thought I was going to faint.

Chapter Nine

"Mom! Are you okay?" Noelle was practically running toward me across the parking lot as I watched the tow truck start to pull my car onto the flatbed.

I turned to her and tried to smile, but I must have been less than successful in appearing fine because she immediately pulled me into a hug.

"It's going to be okay, Mom."

I hugged her back for a long time, glad to have the support. I was pretty freaked out by the warning on my car. Just as I released her and started to step back, I looked over her shoulder and saw the guy from the diner and the coffee shop standing awkwardly a few feet away.

I felt my breath grow shallow with fear, and I hissed into my daughter's ear, "What is he doing here?"

"Who?" she asked, looking over her shoulder. "Oh, Tom. He was at the coffee shop when you called. He offered to come with me in case he could help." She waved him over.

I eyed him suspiciously. He seemed to be showing up everywhere I was. The diner and the coffee shop could just be a coincidence, but then he was at the police station, too. "How long had he been at the coffee shop?" I whispered to Noelle, turning my head away from him so he wouldn't overhear.

She gave me a puzzled glance and said, "At least an hour. Why?"

So, he couldn't have left the threat. I relaxed, and my breathing returned to normal. I wasn't sure why that made me feel so relieved. I shrugged. "Just wondered."

She stared at me for another moment but then decided to let it go.

Tom stepped up and asked tentatively, "Are you doing okay, Ellen?"

I smiled, feeling strangely better with his solid presence next to me. One minute, I suspected him of being the murderer, and the next, I was happy he was here. I must be losing my mind.

"I'm fine. Whoever did this was long gone before I came out here. Just irritated now since I'm without a car," I said, making a face to try to lighten the mood, both for them and myself.

"What do the police say?" he asked, still looking concerned.

"They tried to check and see if there were cameras in the parking lot that might show who did it, but no luck. I guess there was a large SUV parked next to my car that blocked their view. Too bad I don't have a fancy car like yours, with built-in cameras."

He looked startled, but before he could respond, the police chief came out of the retirement center and walked over to us.

"Tom." He nodded at the man I was standing with. "What brings you here?" he asked.

"I was in the coffee shop when Ellen called Noelle and came along with her to see if I could help." The look that passed between the two men seemed to communicate more than just the words that were spoken, but I didn't have the energy at the moment to figure it out. Suddenly, a wave of fatigue washed over me.

"Is it okay for me to head home?" I asked Chief Andrews. "I'm feeling a bit shaky."

"Of course, Ellen," he said. "But remember, from now on, leave the investigating to us. I think if you do as the warning said and stop asking questions, you should be safe, but if anything else happens or you feel unsafe, please feel free to call me." He handed me a business card. "This has my cell phone number on it, so you can reach me anytime."

I thanked him as Noelle came up and started leading me to her car.

"I'll take you home, Mom. Do you want me to stay with you?" she asked.

"No, honey," I said. "I think I'll just take a nap. I'm really tired and a little overwhelmed. Besides, I've already taken you away from work long enough anyway. Your boss isn't going to be happy with me."

"She completely understood why I needed to leave and told me to take all the time I needed, so don't worry about that," Noelle replied, looking concerned. "You sure you want to be alone?"

"I'm sure," I answered, trying to sound more confident than I actually felt. I didn't want to cause Noelle to miss more work on my account.

Tom walked up after talking with the chief for a minute more and heard the last part of the conversation. "I could stay with you if you'd like," he said. "That way, Noelle can go back to work, and you won't be alone. I can bring my computer in and work while you lie down."

I thought about it for a minute. It did sound good to not be alone, but what did I really know about this man?

Before I could respond, Noelle chimed in. "That would be great, Tom! Then I won't worry so much."

How could I say no now, when it was going to keep my daughter from worrying? "Okay," I acquiesced, trying to sound grateful but just feeling exhausted and stressed.

Noelle walked us to Tom's car and then gave me another hug. As she turned to leave, I called out to her, "Noelle, can you go check on Grandma after work tonight? I'm sure she's heard what happened, but I doubt I'll feel like talking on the phone later, and she'll want some assurance that I'm okay."

She nodded her assent and then hurried off to her car to return to work.

Tom showed me how to open the unusual door. I had ridden in a Tesla before, but not one as fancy as this. I gave him my address, and he plugged it into his GPS. "How long have you had your car?" I asked to be polite.

"About six months. I had a Model S before this, but I upgraded to this X when the price came down."

I nodded, too exhausted to talk anymore. That must have been obvious, because Tom didn't try to continue the conversation either. He turned on some classical music, and I found myself drifting as we drove to my house, letting the music wash over me to calm my frayed nerves.

<hr>

Chapter Ten

I was nearly asleep when we reached the house. Tom pulled up just outside the garage, and I used my phone to open it. It was upsetting to see the empty garage where my car should have been. The door from the garage took us into the family room. One end of the room was covered in brick and held a large fireplace with a railroad tie for a mantle. The rest of the walls were plastered at the top with beadboard under a chair rail. It had a large sliding glass door, where I normally let Louisa out into the backyard. Waiting to go out, she was patiently sitting in front of it when I opened the door from the garage, but she started barking when she saw Tom. I quickly introduced them, and Tom let her sniff his hand before scratching her behind her ears.

"You'll be her best friend for life if you keep doing that." I smiled my first genuine smile in the last hour.

He smiled back. "She is a beautiful dog. What kind is she?"

"An American Bulldog/Shar-Pei mix." I opened the slider to let her out and took a big breath of fresh air before turning back to him. I gestured to my gray tweed couch with two dark pine end tables on either side of it. "There is a power strip on the bottom level of the right end table you are welcome to plug into, or if you prefer a table, the breakfast nook is right this way."

I led him through a large opening into a dining area and a large country kitchen. The table was a built-in, banquette style, with dark-green faux-leather seats. There was a large kitchen island that contained my cooktop and oven, along with a bar with three barstools. The sink was under a garden window where I somewhat unsuccessfully grew some small herbs. The refrigerator was on the opposite wall next to floor-to-ceiling cabinets that I used as a pantry.

I opened the pantry door and showed Tom where I kept my snacks. "Feel free to help yourself to anything you see here or in the refrigerator. If you wouldn't mind letting Louisa in when she comes back to the door, I think I have to go lie down now." I had been getting more and more tired, and I felt myself shutting down.

"You go ahead," Tom said. "Don't worry about me. I'll take care of Louisa and get some work done. You get some rest." His tone was warm and soothing.

I dragged myself to my room on the other end of the house and collapsed on my bed, practically asleep before my head hit the pillow.

Suddenly, I was back on the path, staring at the fallen limb, only this time I could hear Natalie calling out for help. No matter how I tried, I couldn't get to her. Then I saw someone coming from behind the tree. I couldn't tell who it was because he had a mask over his face. I saw him reaching for Natalie, and I screamed for help.

I startled awake with the echo of my scream still in the air. My heart was racing, and I was covered in a cold sweat, like I had been running in my sleep.

Tom burst into the room. "Are you okay?" He looked around frantically, as if someone might be hiding in my room.

"I'm okay," I said, sitting up. "Just another bad dream."

"Another?" he asked.

"I've been having them ever since I found Natalie's body," I said, trying to sound calm, although the dreams always left me feeling unsettled and afraid. I pulled my legs up and hugged my knees. "They aren't all the same, but in all of them, I keep trying to save her, and I can't get to her. Sometimes I see the killer coming to finish the job, and sometimes I get to her, only to have her die just as I figure out a way to get past the tree. The only common denominator is that I fail to save her." I felt wrung out and no more rested than when I went to sleep.

He sat down on the edge of the bed and looked me in the eye with compassion. "I'm sorry you're going through this. You know you couldn't have saved her no matter what you did when you reached the tree, right? She was already dead, from everything I've heard."

"I know that in my head when I'm awake, but when I'm asleep, my mind apparently doesn't believe those facts." I groaned wearily.

"Have you actually been investigating?" he asked, looking at me with an intensity I couldn't quite understand, but his eyes were mesmerizing, so I couldn't look away.

"Not exactly. At least, I didn't set out to, but I keep running into people involved, or people tell me things they've heard, and I can't help my curiosity. Plus, I want to help Frankie, and I feel like I owe it to Natalie to find the truth," I said weakly as he frowned at me.

"You know what they say curiosity did to the cat," he said warningly, and I blanched, my mind flashing to the warning on my car with the red paint dripping down like blood. "Oh no, Ellen, I'm so sorry!" He reached out and took my hand, squeezing it in his. "I didn't mean to frighten you more. I just want you to be careful." His hand warmed my freezing one, and I didn't want him to let go.

Suddenly, I realized that I was sitting on my bed with a stranger holding my hand, and I pulled away. "I think I need something to drink." I got up from the bed and slipped on my shoes. "Would you like some hot or iced tea or...?" I raised my eyebrows to indicate something else.

He stood and smiled sheepishly. Apparently, the situation had struck him, too. "Not much into tea, but if you have something diet, I'd take that."

I led the way into the kitchen and put the kettle on while I got him a drink from the fridge. He declined a glass of ice and sat down at the table while I fussed around making tea and feeling awkward.

I finally sat down and decided that if he was free to ask me questions, then I could ask him some too. "So, what brings you to Cascade?" I tried to sound casual while I contemplated what I might learn from this man.

"I was looking for a change of pace," he answered.

"From what?" I asked, even more curious because of the lack of details in his answer.

"I've had a very high-pressure job for the last twenty years, and it was starting to affect my health." Again, he didn't elaborate.

"I get that." I decided that maybe if I shared some of my story, he might be more comfortable opening up to me. "I just retired from a career as a child labor investigator. Worked at the same place for thirty years. It could be very high pressure, especially when we were doing targeted enforcement. Now I'm trying to figure out what I want to do next. I'm not ready to sit around and play bingo like my mom," I said, laughing a bit. "So, what did you do?" I hoped that this time he would open up a bit more.

"I was on a federal task force investigating cybercrimes," he said almost reluctantly.

"Wow!" I exclaimed in awe. "I had to take annual security training every year for my job. I can understand why you would feel stressed. So, are you just taking a break or moving on to something new?"

He shrugged. "I'm working on what I hope will be my last case now, and then I can move on to something else." He'd unbent just a little but immediately seemed to clam up again. I wondered if he regretted telling me even that much.

After that, the conversation was stilted, with me asking questions and him responding in monosyllables. I didn't have the energy to keep trying this hard to get to know him, so I decided it was time for him to go.

"Look," I finally said. "I appreciate you staying while I napped, but I'm sure you have better things to do than babysit me. I'll lock up when you leave and stay right here. I'm sure I'll be fine." I hoped I sounded more confident than I was feeling.

While I was ready to be alone and think things through, I was still a little freaked out about the warning on my car.

He seemed reluctant to agree, which surprised me. This hot and cold stuff was sending me very mixed signals. He finally left after I told him I would text Noelle and let her know he was leaving.

"Whew," I said aloud. He made my head spin. When he'd come into my room after the nightmare, he'd been caring and seemed to really want to be with me, but just a few minutes later, he'd gone totally cold. I knew it had been a while since I was in a relationship, but surely I couldn't be misreading the signals this badly. I sighed.

I peeked out of the curtains to watch him back down my drive. Just as I turned away to start something for dinner, I caught a flash out of the corner of my eye. Could someone else be out there? Maybe staying here alone was a bad idea.

Chapter Eleven

"Thanks for coming to get me, Lisa." I hugged the petite blonde with enormous blue eyes. We had been friends since the first day of kindergarten and knew each other practically better than we knew ourselves.

"Why didn't you call me sooner?" she asked, exasperated. "I go out of town for a few days, and all hell breaks loose with my best friend. If I hadn't stopped at the coffee shop, I would have had no idea anything was going on. Good thing Noelle filled me in so I wasn't totally in the dark when you called," she continued while dragging my suitcase out to her car. She was stronger than she looked, thanks to her regular workouts. Unlike me, she was good about cardio and lifting weights, and it showed when she lifted my heavy suitcase like it was a feather.

I had decided that while I might be jumping at shadows, I doubted I would feel safe staying in my house by myself, with no car and no close neighbors. I'd called Lisa and asked if I could stay with her and her husband, Mike, for a few days until I got my car back. They lived in town, so I could walk over to see Noelle and my mother easily, and Mike was a tall, burly, former drill sergeant who looked like he could play linebacker for the pros. He was a bit obsessive about security, so I doubted there was a safer place I could be than at their house.

I snapped the leash onto Louisa's collar and headed for Lisa's car. "Are you sure you're okay with Lou staying with you?" I asked. "I'm sure Noelle could take her for a few days."

"It's fine," she assured me while she covered the back seat with a blanket. "Don't you think you would feel safer having her with you?"

I nodded. She was right, of course, but I hated to put Lisa out. Louisa could be a handful at times. Louisa jumped up into the back seat and sat. She was one of those weird dogs who didn't stick her head out the window, so I got her to lie down before closing the door. "Okay, but if she gets to be too much, please don't hesitate to tell me," I implored her.

As we started toward town, I kept my eye out for anything that would indicate someone had been in the woods next to my driveway, but I didn't see anything that looked unusual. The problem was that there were so many trees, it would be easy for someone to hide out and remain completely invisible from the road.

"So, Noelle told me what she knew, but if I know you, she doesn't know the whole story. Time to spill." Lisa glanced over with a look that said she would know if I left anything out.

I told her about everything that had happened.

"Oh my gosh!" she interjected when I told her about the tires being slashed and the threat. "What on earth did you stumble into? I didn't think Cascade had murders and threats. We're just a little town, not the big city! A few tricks on Halloween is the most I thought we ever had."

"I guess evil can exist anywhere, even in a small town," I replied. "But even so, I don't understand why someone would want to threaten me. I haven't found out that much. And why kill Natalie? She was so nice."

"Mike knows her fiancé," Lisa said. "He had some business with him a few months ago. I wouldn't call him a friend, but they've had coffee a few times when they ran into each other at The Grounds."

"Really," I said, considering. "I may want to talk to Mike about him when we get to your house."

She gave me the side-eye. "I thought you were going to back off. A killer threatened you! What are you *thinking*?"

"I'm not sure I'm going to be safe until this person is caught," I said, turning to look at her. "I want to feel safe in my house again, and I'm not sure that's possible until the right person is arrested."

"Isn't that why we have the police?" she asked, sounding exasperated. "They *are* the professionals."

"But they seem to be looking at the wrong people. I mean, they've focused on Frankie's brother, Tony. Are they even looking at other suspects?" I started listing all my unanswered questions. "Why was she in the park? I think she was meeting someone, but who? And why?"

Lisa groaned. "Okay, I admit those are good questions, but why do you have to be the one to answer them?"

"Because I don't know that anyone else is asking them," I replied, and we lapsed into silence until we got to the house.

Mike came out the door when we pulled into their garage and grabbed my bag out of the trunk. "You okay?" he asked, giving me a side hug as he passed me to lead the way into their game room. There was a large stone fireplace at one end of the room with a wooden game table surrounded by comfy chairs in front of it. We passed through into the combined kitchen/dining room.

I plopped down on a barstool at the large center island and groaned. "I'm better now that I'm here."

"I'm surprised you went home at all after the threat," Lisa said as she walked into the room. "I wouldn't have wanted to be alone out there for a minute."

"I guess Noelle failed to tell you that I wasn't alone." I grinned at their reactions when I told them about Mr. Tall, Dark, and Handsome coming over to watch over me.

"That sounds like Tom Green," Mike said. "Is he tall with brown hair graying at the temples?"

"That's him."

"I think I met him before we went on our trip. Seemed like a nice guy. A little intense."

"Definitely," I said. "He does seem nice, but I can't figure him out." I shook my head.

Lisa perked up. "What does that mean? Are you interested in him?"

"I don't know. Maybe," I said, shrugging. "Hard to tell at this point, but it doesn't matter since I don't think he's interested in me."

"Of course he is," Lisa said positively.

"You haven't even met him," I scoffed. "How could you possibly know?"

"A man doesn't come and watch over you while you sleep if he isn't interested in you," she said knowingly.

I waved her off and changed the subject. "Hey, Mike... Lisa tells me you know Max Holland. What do you know about him?"

"He's a high-powered attorney down in the city. Works at one of those big firms right downtown. I met him at a business owners' luncheon when he spoke about the pros and cons of accepting cryptocurrency," Mike replied.

"Cryptocurrency?" I asked, flabbergasted. "People try to pay small businesses in cryptocurrency?"

Mike replied, "Not often, but occasionally someone asks. I don't want to mess with it, but I know some people see it as a good business practice."

"I know absolutely nothing about bitcoin or any of the others," I said. "It always seems so nebulous to me. I mean, how is there virtual money that just exists on the web somewhere?"

"I don't understand it completely myself," Mike replied. "But from hearing Max's talk, it seems like there's a record of transactions called a blockchain. The blockchain records information about the transaction, like who is making it, and so on. Its value is determined by the market, just like stocks and bonds. If you want to know more, you should talk to Max. He does a great job of explaining it."

"I just may do that," I murmured, thinking a conversation with Max might shed a lot more light on what was going on, and not just about cryptocurrency.

Chapter Twelve

settled in to spend the night in the guest room, which Lisa had decorated in beige and gray with dark-green accents. It was soothing and comfortable, with a queen-size bed, a wooden rocking chair, and an en suite with a tub/shower combo. I put my toiletries in the bath and went right to sleep, still exhausted from the events of the day.

When I woke up the next morning, I was feeling more relaxed. After a good night's sleep, the fear of the previous day seemed to be a bit of an overreaction. Especially with the sun shining brightly through the windows, indicating it was going to be a beautiful day. I found a note from Lisa on the counter downstairs, telling me to feel free to hang out as long as I wanted. She and Mike would be at work all day, but Mike was close by if I needed him.

I decided to take Louisa for a walk. I was a bit reluctant to go back to the trails at Cascade Falls Park, but I was afraid that if I delayed too long, I'd never get myself to go back again. Plus, it was within walking distance, and I didn't want to bother anyone for a ride, since I knew they were all at work.

It was a short walk to the park from Lisa's, and I cut through the playground to get to the bridge over the falls. I decided to take the trail the opposite way from what I normally did. I would start at the falls and end at the parking lot. I was hoping that by going the other way, I would be less nervous about being back.

Louisa, as usual, was raring to go, and I had a hard time getting her to pause on the bridge over the falls. But I needed the time to let the sound of the water calm me. I had a feeling of dread at going back into the woods here, and watching the water helped me let go of stress and negative thoughts. It wasn't a very high waterfall, but it made up for that in the power of the water coming over the rocks. It always reminded me that I was just a drop of water being rushed along by the current of life, and it was only God's power that kept me from being overwhelmed. I said a quick prayer for peace and that I would not let fear keep me from enjoying nature, and then I finally let Louisa drag me off the bridge to the trailhead.

It was harder starting from here, as the first part of the trail was very steeply uphill, but once at the top, we were enveloped by lush foliage that dampened the sound of the children playing at the park. Even the falls were somewhat muted up here among the trees. I wondered if that was why no one had heard anything when Natalie was murdered. Surely she'd fought her attacker! If it were me, I would have screamed my head off, but if no one was very close, the sound might not have carried.

Of course, if her murderer was someone she knew well, they might have taken her off guard. Would I scream if someone I cared about came up to talk to me on my walk? Probably not, unless they startled me. So maybe she hadn't screamed. *Oh, Natalie... I wish I could know what you were thinking and seeing. I want so much to get justice for you.* There were so many unanswered questions, and I felt powerless to find the answers.

As we moved along the path, I kept an eye out for any place the branch could have come from. I saw a couple of places where there were some fallen limbs, but none were comparable in size to the one used to make Natalie's death look like an accident. The forest was dense here, so it was possible someone could have forced their way deeper into the forest to find one. That thought made me nervous, and I was already feeling jumpy just being back in these woods. I could feel my heart rate elevating, and it wasn't just from the exercise.

Just then, the sun went behind a cloud, making the woods even darker. While it was never bright under the trees, there were normally areas where the sun shone through and made leaf shadows on the trail. But now it was dark and felt foreboding in a way I'd never experienced there before. I knew it was probably all in my head, but I picked up the pace anyway, hearing the crunch of leaves under my feet as I hurried. Just around the next bend, I reached the point where I'd found Natalie. There was some leftover yellow police tape hanging limply along one side of the trail, so I knew it was the right spot if I'd had any doubt. I would have known that was where I was anyway, though. This place was implanted in my memory, and I doubted I would ever forget it. Someone had also left a teddy bear with a small bouquet near where the tree branch had been dragged off the trail.

I bent down to see if there was any indication of who had left it. The bear had a bright-red bow on it, and the flowers were also red. It made me wonder if that was Natalie's favorite color. It couldn't have been here very long since the flowers were still fresh, despite not being in water. There was a card attached, but it was difficult to read in the gloom. I finally pulled out my cell phone and turned on the flashlight so I could see what it said.

You should have minded your own business was printed in bold black letters, but there was no signature. Could this have been from the killer? I suddenly stood up and looked all around me, my breath coming in gasps, paranoid that someone was watching me. I didn't see anyone or hear anything, but my heart was pounding in my throat, and my fight-or-flight instinct kicked in.

"Come on, Louisa." I tugged on her leash to make her come back from whatever she had found so interesting in the underbrush. We hurried down the trail for a couple of hundred more yards until Louisa stopped dead and started growling low in her throat, staring at a place in the woods a few feet in front of us. That was it. I was done with this walk. I quickly turned around and went back the way we had come as fast as I could.

By the time we hit the place where Natalie was found, I was practically running. My heartbeat was so loud, I couldn't hear if anyone was following us, but I wasn't waiting around to find out. I didn't really feel safe until we got back to the bridge. Thankfully, there were people everywhere around the falls area, enjoying the sunshine, which I noticed had come back out from behind the clouds. I paused on the bridge again to catch my breath.

What was I thinking, going back out into those woods with a killer on the loose? Reclaiming my favorite trail was going to have to wait until this murder was solved. And even then, I doubted I would ever find it as relaxing as I used to. We walked the rest of the way back to Lisa's while my heart slowed, but I couldn't suppress the itchy feeling down my back that someone was watching us.

Chapter Thirteen

was still feeling restless when we got back to the house, so after giving Louisa some water and a treat, I decided to head back downtown to The Grounds to see Noelle.

I left Louisa happily playing in their large fenced-in backyard and started for the coffee shop. I hadn't gone more than a block when I ran into Tara coming out of an old Victorian house that had been beautifully restored. It was white with green and burgundy accents and had stained glass around the edge of the windows in the front-facing rooms downstairs. There was a wide covered porch with a white wicker couch and several rocking chairs, as well as tables scattered around. Best of all was the porch swing hanging at one end.

"Oh, hi, Tara!" I smiled at her. "Is this where you live? It's beautiful. I bet you love sitting out on that porch."

She grinned wearily. "Yes. I've been fixing it up myself in my free time, but with Natalie gone, I'm not sure when I'll get back to it. Running the shop by myself is exhausting." She sighed.

"Oh, Tara, I'm so sorry. I'm sure that's a lot. Do you have any help at all?" I asked.

"I have a couple of part-time high school girls who come in after school and on weekends, but they can't really help with opening and closing the store, and I don't think they're ready to do things like deposits. I guess I could hire someone else, but I really would like to have a partner. It's so much nicer to have someone to bounce ideas off of and share the responsibility with." She teared up a little as she obviously thought of Natalie.

"You know, I've been thinking for a while about what I want to do with myself. I might be interested in talking more about this when you have some time." I felt a surge of excitement bubble up at the thought.

"Really?" she exclaimed, brightening. "I would love to sit down and discuss it as soon as the cloud of Natalie's murder is no longer hanging over me."

We started walking toward downtown together, as we were both heading the same way.

"Have you heard anything about the investigation?" I asked after we had gone a few steps, hoping she knew more than I did.

She frowned. "It seems that I'm now under suspicion. The chief came to talk to me yesterday. I guess someone must have overheard my argument with Natalie, and now he thinks I might have killed her!"

I winced, knowing I was the someone she was referring to. "Oh no! I'm so sorry, Tara! Were you able to convince him you didn't do it?"

"Sort of. I told him I had gone straight to Frankie's to eat after the argument, so someone should be able to verify I was there, but I guess they aren't sure yet exactly what time she was killed, so that may not help me," she bemoaned.

We paused at a stoplight. "I hope everything works out okay and we can talk once this is all resolved." I impulsively reached out and hugged her as the light changed. "I'll let you go since I know you're really busy."

"We'll talk soon," she said with determination as she turned to go to her store.

I turned the other way to head to The Grounds. I hoped she would bounce back once the truth about Natalie's death came out—assuming she wasn't the killer, though I didn't really think she was. Something in my gut said the answer was more complicated than a simple crime of passion.

A few more blocks, and I stepped into the coffee shop to see my daughter deep in conversation with a man I didn't know. He looked to be in his mid-thirties and was way overdressed for our casual little town at this time of morning. He had on an expensive gray suit with a matching paisley tie and pocket square. I heard her say, "I'm so sorry for your loss."

I realized this must be Max, Natalie's fiancé. As he turned to leave, I got a better look at him. Dark hair and piercing hazel eyes, which looked more angry than grief-stricken, highlighted an angular face. He had the same runner's body that Natalie had had—lean and lanky. He brushed past me without even glancing my way, but the look on his face had me recoiling.

As the door closed after him, the room seemed to exhale, as if it had been holding its breath.

I turned to my daughter. "He seems forceful!"

Noelle shrugged. "He's always like that. Maybe just a bit more so now that he doesn't have Natalie. I always felt like she softened him."

"Did they come in here often?" I asked. "I didn't recognize him, and I'm in here all the time, so I'm surprised I haven't run into them."

"They'd normally come in later in the evening, close to closing time, and you're normally here during the day," she answered. "How are you this morning? I'm glad you didn't stay at your place alone last night!"

"I'm doing okay—wondering if I overreacted," I answered with a little half-smile. "Although without a car, I would have felt trapped at home. At least this way I can walk wherever I need to go in town. I did freak myself out this morning, though, when I took Louisa for a walk in the park." I told her about finding the memorial on the trail and Louisa growling at something.

She started making my hot chocolate just the way I like it. "That would have creeped me out, too. I don't want you minimizing this. Someone damaged your car as a warning. Don't forget that! I'm glad you're staying with Mike and Lisa and aren't alone out there at the house," she said sternly, handing me my cup. "Do you know when you'll get your car back?"

"I called this morning, and it's going to be a couple of more days." I sighed. "Once the police finished processing it, I had it towed to the shop. Apparently, the tires were all damaged beyond repair, and they had to order new ones. They won't be in until late tomorrow. I hate feeling like I'm stuck at home for that long, so I guess I'll stay with Lisa at least until I get my car back."

"Good!" She smiled, seeming relieved that I would be staying with someone. "If you need a ride somewhere or need to borrow my car, I'm working here a lot this week since we're on break from school, so just ask if you need it."

"Thanks, honey!" I smiled back at her. "Enough about my problems. Anything interesting going on with you?"

I saw something flicker behind her eyes, but it was gone before I could figure it out. *Hmmm.*

"Same old, same old," she said nonchalantly, and if I hadn't seen the flicker, I would have believed her.

"What was Max being so emphatic about with you before he left?" I asked, deciding to change the subject. Pressure never got my daughter to open up about anything.

"That was weird," she replied, seeming so relieved I'd moved on to a different subject that she answered more quickly than she normally would have. "He was insisting that he left something in here the other day when he was in, but we haven't found anything like what he was describing. He seemed to think someone might have taken it. He brought up Tom."

"Tom!" I exclaimed. "How does he know Tom? And why would he think Tom would have taken whatever it is?"

"He doesn't actually know Tom, but the person he described could only be Tom. He said he saw him sitting at the table where he and Natalie normally sit. Wanted his contact information. As if we keep records for all our customers." She rolled her eyes. "He was being so pushy about it that I didn't even tell him Tom's name. I wish I could say this was the first time he'd acted strangely in here, but it isn't. A few weeks ago, he and Natalie were in, and he seemed to be interrogating her, like it was one of his trials and she was on the witness stand."

"Did you hear what he was asking her about?" I asked, frowning.

"Something about whether she had been in his study at home. She denied being in there and started to get up and leave, but he grabbed her wrist and pulled her back down into her chair. He talked really quietly to her then, so I don't know what he said, but when Tara came in looking for her, she jumped right up and practically ran out of here." She shook her head. "I thought I was going to have to call the police, but he didn't try to stop her when she left."

"Do you think he hurt her arm when he pulled her down?" She shrugged.

"By the way... What exactly did he lose?" I asked.

"A flash drive," she replied. "He said it had confidential information on it, and it must have fallen out of his pocket, but then he went on a rant about someone taking it. I think he's close to snapping."

Chapter Fourteen

bunch of people came in just then, so I left Noelle to wait on them and found a quiet table in the corner. I thought about what she had said while I sipped my hot chocolate. What could be on the flash drive that was so important? Was it client records? I bet that could get him in trouble since they're supposed to be confidential. But why would he think someone had taken it? Mostly, why would he think it was Tom? The next time I saw that man, I was going to have more questions.

It felt like my list of questions was getting longer instead of shorter. I wasn't sure I had any answers at all. I decided I should check in with my mom and let her see in person that I was okay. I had had Noelle reassure her yesterday after the incident with my car, but I knew she would worry until she saw me in person.

I hugged my daughter goodbye, grabbed my coat, and headed out.

As I walked over to the retirement center, I thought through the questions I had listed in my notebook:

1. Did Natalie go jogging to blow off some steam after the argument with Tara?

I still had no idea about this one.

1. What did Tara mean about Natalie's fiancé not treating her right? Was he abusive?

I wondered if she was referring to the coffee shop incident. The fact that Natalie was considering breaking things off with him lent some credence to this. As did the anger I saw in him at The Grounds, Noelle's story about him grabbing Natalie's wrist, and her comment about him being on the edge of "losing it."

1. Why did the police suspect Frankie's brother, Tony, over her current fiancé?

Finally, one I had some answers for. Natalie had been spending time with Tony, and he wanted her to take him back. Everything I'd heard made it sound like she was happy to have Tony back in her life, but she could have rejected him again, and that set him off.

1. If the tree didn't kill Natalie, what did kill her?

I still didn't have any idea how to find this out. Maybe Becky could tell me something, but I wouldn't want to jeopardize her job. I'd have to think about that.

1. What exactly did Noelle hear from people about Tara, Tony, and Natalie's fiancé, Max? Did she tell me everything she'd heard?

Maybe it wasn't so much what she heard, but more what she saw herself. I'd have to ask her the next time I saw her.

I paused to add my new questions to the list:

1. What was on the flash drive, and where is it now?

2. Why did Max think Tom might have it?

3. Who left the memorial on the trail?

Satisfied that I had done all I could at the moment, I hurried on to see my mom. When I went to her room, I found it empty. I checked the activity calendar on her refrigerator to see if I could figure out where she was. No luck, so I started checking all the common spaces. I found her playing cards in the activity room.

It was a utilitarian room that reminded me of a school lunchroom. There were several six-foot tables set up with chairs, and a counter at one end with a refrigerator, sink, and cabinets above and below. On another wall were floor-to-ceiling bookshelves with books, puzzles, games, and movies. Under the window was a table with some partially completed puzzles on it. They had activities here all day long, and when there were no scheduling conflicts, a set of the residents often played cards. Mom was a sub with the group instead of a regular, as her hearing had been getting worse. Apparently, today she was filling in.

"Ellen," she shouted. "Are you okay?" I smiled to reassure her, but she went on before I could answer. "I was hoping you would be coming by today. If you hadn't come, I'd have called. Come hear what Martha saw," she said, pointing at one of the other ladies at the table.

I walked up, gave Mom a quick hug, and sat down on a nearby chair. Today she was wearing brown pants, a leaf-printed blouse, and a long brown cardigan. Of course, she had on her signature pearls. "Hi, Mom." I nodded hello to all the other ladies playing cards.

"Martha!" Mom impatiently waved her hands in the air. "Tell her about the man you saw."

Martha, a little white-haired lady who was so petite she looked like a strong wind would blow her over, looked up at me shyly. "Now, Carol, I didn't really see anything much."

My mom frowned fiercely at her, so she continued. "It was just that I went out shopping with my daughter yesterday, and as we were coming back, I saw a man in the parking lot. When I heard about what happened to your car, I wondered if maybe he might have been the one who did it."

"What did he look like?" I asked, hoping her description would help identify the man who had threatened me and damaged my car.

"Well, you know my eyesight isn't what it used to be," she started, pointing at her thick glasses.

My mom jumped in. "You told me he was tall and good-looking."

"That's true," said Martha.

"What color hair did he have?" I asked, hoping to get more details.

"Dark," she answered promptly, clearly excited that she'd remembered that detail.

"Was he slim or muscular?" I asked.

She frowned. "I don't really know. He had on bulky clothes, all black, and I couldn't tell much more than that he was tall."

"That's okay," I reassured her. I didn't want her to feel bad about not having more details. This was more than anyone else had seen.

I sat and thought as they went back to playing their card game. That description certainly didn't narrow it down. Max, Tom, and even the police chief were all tall with dark hair. So much for narrowing it down. I suddenly had a thought.

"Martha, do you think you would recognize him if you saw a picture?" I asked, and all of them turned to stare at me.

She shrugged. "Maybe?"

I pulled up Facebook and looked at Natalie's page for a picture of Max. I showed the best one I could find to Martha.

"I'm not sure. It could be him. I'm just not sure."

I didn't have a picture of Tom to show her and didn't know of any mutual friends I could use to Facebook-stalk him. I guess I'd just have to be careful around both of them.

I realized that while I was thinking, they had gone back to their card game and their conversation, and I caught Natalie's name, but not the context.

"Tomorrow is sooner than I thought it would be," one of the other ladies said.

"I'm sorry," I said, interrupting again. "What's tomorrow?"

"Natalie's funeral," my mom informed me. "Frankie's aunt Anita told us. I guess they released Tony, and he's planning to be there."

"I'm glad to hear he was released, but I suspect Max won't be too happy to see him at the funeral."

They broke into conversation about it, all talking over each other. I decided I had interrupted their card game enough and hugged Mom before slipping out of the room and leaving them to their game. I had a lot to think about as I headed back to Lisa's house.

Chapter Fifteen

s I was walking back to Lisa's house, I found myself passing the police station and decided that I should tell Chief Andrews about what Martha had seen, even if it wasn't much to go on. I was sort of hoping he might share some more information about the investigation, but I didn't have high hopes.

The chief was standing at the front desk when I walked in and quickly ushered me back to his office, so I didn't have a chance to talk with Becky, who waved at me as I walked by.

"To what do I owe this unexpected pleasure?" he asked dryly. "No further warnings?" he continued more seriously, searching me with his blue-eyed gaze.

"No." I shook my head. "No further warnings. Well, at least not directed at me," I said, thinking of the card on the bouquet in the park. "I'm staying with Lisa and Mike Partridge here in town while my car gets repaired. I walked over to see my mother at the retirement home." I proceeded to tell him about what Martha had said. "Unfortunately, her description could fit a lot of people, so I'm not sure how much it helps, but since

I was passing the police station, I decided to stop in and let you know."

"Maybe her daughter saw more than Martha did," he said thoughtfully. "I'll reach out to her and see what she has to say. Thank you for bringing this to my attention instead of pursuing it yourself." Again, he speared me with his penetrating gaze. "But what did you mean 'at least not directed at me'?" he asked, holding my gaze.

I told him about the teddy bear and flowers on the trail and what the card said.

"Hm!" He looked thoughtful. "Did you see anyone out there on the trail?"

"No, but Louisa stopped and started growling at something ahead of us in the woods, so we turned around and got out of there."

He grinned. "So you do have some sense of self-preservation. I was beginning to wonder."

I bit my tongue to keep from responding hotly and stood up to leave. I turned back. "I guess I'll see you at the funeral tomorrow. I hope there won't be trouble there."

"Why would there be trouble at the funeral?" he asked sharply.

"I heard that Tony was planning to come. I hope that doesn't cause trouble with Max," I replied.

"Now, where did you hear that?" he asked.

"The retirement home," I answered with a laugh. "There is very little that goes on in this town that they don't know about, and they hear things faster than they can be posted on social media."

For the first time since I arrived, he relaxed. "Some of those older ladies would have made great spies or detectives. Maybe I should put them on the payroll. I'll have several officers present at the funeral, and I'll be there myself. We'll make sure there's no trouble."

I left his office and started down the hall to leave before remembering that I still hadn't asked about Louisa's bowl and my water bottle. I went back to ask the chief, but when I approached his door, I heard him speaking to someone.

"So, what kind of blade do you think caused the wounds?"

When no one responded that I could hear, I realized he was on the phone.

"Uh-huh. I see. Like a letter opener?"

I backed away. I didn't want the chief to think I had been eavesdropping.

I decided to see if Becky was back at her desk to get Lou's bowl. I now knew how Natalie had been killed. She'd been stabbed! I hadn't seen any blood at the scene that I could recall. Shouldn't there have been a lot of blood if she'd been stabbed? Maybe she hadn't been killed where I'd found her.

I was still pondering this new information when I walked up to Becky's desk. "Hey, do you know if they found my water bottle and Louisa's bowl out in the woods the day I found Natalie?" I asked Becky.

"I'm not sure. No one said anything, but they may be back with the evidence. If they are, I'm not sure if I can give them to you or not. Let me check with the chief." Becky headed back down the hall from where I had just come.

I leaned on the counter in front of her desk and happened to glance down at what was on her computer screen. I wasn't sure exactly what I was seeing, but it looked like Becky was typing up people's statements. I looked around to make sure no one was paying attention to me and that Becky was still back with the chief, and then I leaned over a bit more to see if I could see what papers were on her desk. I'd been correct. It looked like handwritten statements. I could just make out a bit on the lower part of the first page of the top statement, but where the name should be was covered by another piece of paper. I considered trying to ease the other paper out of the way, but I was too short to reach it.

I decided to focus on what I could read and figure out later whose statement it was. It read:

...dinner that night, and she was really nervous. She was really upset with something Max had done, and she said she had decided to break off her engagement with him. I asked her what he had done, but she said she didn't want to put me in danger, and she had already found the right person to tell who could do something about it. I was concerned about her putting herself in danger, but she assured me everything would be okay by the next afternoon. I didn't want her to go back to her apartment with Max that night, but she insisted I drop her off.

That was all I'd gotten when I heard footsteps approaching and straightened up so they wouldn't see what I had been doing. It was Becky and Chief Andrews. As Becky slid behind her desk, Chief Andrews began apologizing.

"I'm sorry, Ellen, but since your water bottle and Louisa's bowl were collected as evidence at the crime scene and this is an active investigation, I can't return them to you yet. You should get them back once we have someone in custody and we've established that they won't be needed as evidence at trial."

"I figured as much," I said with a shrug. "Thank you."

Becky said, "I'll call you later and check in, Ellen."

When I looked at her, she flicked her gaze down toward her desk.

I smiled and said, "Thanks, Becky. Talk to you later." Nodding once at the chief, I added, "Chief." Then I turned and headed out the door.

I was almost vibrating with the new information I'd learned. Becky had obviously seen me snooping, and she'd moved the paper covering the top of the statement I'd read.

Tony's name had been at the top of the page.

Chapter Sixteen

The next morning, I dressed in a gray and black sheath dress with a matching jacket and chunky-heeled black pumps so I wouldn't have to worry about sinking into the grass at the cemetery. Lisa and Mike were going too, so I rode with them to the church. It was a chilly, overcast day that seemed appropriate for a funeral. I felt anxious and sad. Funerals always reminded me of my husband's, and I rarely attended them for that reason.

The church was an older stone building with large stained-glass windows in various colors that created abstract patterns on the walls when the sun was shining. The large sanctuary could seat several hundred, and I was surprised to find that the church was already very full when we arrived. It was still quite a while before the service, so I expected it would be standing room only by the time it started. Natalie had been well-liked in our community, and I was glad to see that people had come to honor her. I hoped that would comfort her family in some way. I nodded to Chief Andrews, who was stationed near the door.

I hadn't seen Frankie or Tony yet, so I was hoping she'd talked him out of coming. Near the casket at the front of the room, I saw Tara in a tailored black dress with a gray lace scarf around her neck, standing with an older couple I assumed were Natalie's parents. They were both dressed conservatively, but her mom had that same effortless style I had always admired in Natalie, and I knew now where she had gotten it from. I hadn't met them before, but when I asked, Lisa said she knew Natalie's mother from the library board. Alone at the other end of the casket stood Max, in a black suit and a black tie with a small red pattern. I wondered if Natalie had chosen it for him.

Just as we reached the front to offer our condolences to Natalie's parents, I heard Tara say, "Oh no! What is he doing here?"

I turned and saw Frankie and Tony just coming through the door. It didn't take long for Max to notice them, too, and he started down the aisle toward them. Before he got to Tony, I saw the chief step in front of Max and start talking rapidly. Another officer stopped Tony and Frankie and started escorting them toward the stairs to the balcony. Tony seemed reluctant to go, but Frankie grabbed his arm and pulled him to the stairs.

The chief walked Max back to the front, and as they turned around, Max's face was bright red, and he seemed to be struggling to calm down. It reminded me of the look on his face at the coffee shop yesterday.

I turned back to Tara and said, "I take it there's no love lost there." I gestured toward Max and then Tony.

"The feeling seems to go both ways from what Natalie said," she responded in a low voice.

I nodded and then stepped forward for Lisa to introduce me to Natalie's parents. After offering our condolences, we all stepped over to Max, where Mike introduced Lisa and me.

"I'm so sorry," I said. "She was a wonderful person. I wish there had been something I could have done when I found her."

At my words, Max really looked at me for the first time. "You found her?" he asked.

"Yes," I answered sadly. "I was out walking my dog on the trails, and we found her." I shook my head at the memory of that day. "I called 911 right away, but it was already too late."

"You didn't see anyone else out there that day, did you?" he asked.

I shook my head. "No, just a few squirrels and birds. There were lots of cars, but I didn't see anyone else."

He sighed. "Too bad. It might have shed light on who killed her." The words sounded sincere, but the look in his eyes was strange.

We excused ourselves to let the next people step up to speak to him and found a seat about midway back.

The church was completely full by the time the service started. I glanced up at the balcony and saw Frankie and Tony sitting in the front row. Tony had a look of utter despair on his face as he looked at the casket. This was a man who was clearly grieving. But was it because he was denied the chance to win Natalie back or because he killed her? I really didn't want to believe he could have done it, but there must be a reason the police suspected him over the others. If I got a chance later, I needed to talk to him.

It was a beautiful service. The music soared from the pipe organ for the congregational hymns. The pastor clearly knew Natalie well, and his sermon was filled with warm anecdotes and stories her family had shared with him. When he finished, he invited Tara forward to speak.

She stood behind the podium for a minute, just gazing out at the congregation. Then she took a deep breath and straightened her shoulders. "Natalie was my first friend. We met in preschool in the basement of this church and were inseparable from that moment on. We lived three doors down and across the street from each other. Our moms would stand outside and help us cross the street when we went to play together until we were old enough to cross by ourselves. We decorated our bikes for the Fourth of July parade and rode them in it every year until we started high school. We were cheerleaders together and doubles partners in tennis. We double-dated for prom and were college roommates. I always assumed we would be each other's maids of honor at our weddings." She choked up and couldn't continue for a minute. "And I assumed we would be godmothers to each other's children."

At this point, there wasn't a dry eye in the entire church, and I felt tears pouring down my face.

She continued, "Natalie, I know you are in heaven, but I grieve for all the things you never got to experience, that we didn't get to experience together. You leave a hole in my life that no one else will ever fill."

At that, she broke down completely, and the pastor came up and led her to a seat before concluding with prayer.

I thought it was interesting that Max didn't speak, and I wondered if her parents hadn't asked him or if he hadn't wanted to. When we filed past the front row on the way out of the sanctuary, he had his head down and didn't acknowledge anyone who was offering him condolences with more than a nod here and there.

We stopped and spoke to a few people we knew before we headed out to our car and joined the procession to the cemetery. As we were gathering by the tent, I slid up next to Frankie and hugged her. "I know this has to be hard for you," I whispered. I could tell she had been crying.

"She was like family to me. Even after she and Tony broke up, we remained close." She took a shaky breath, clearly trying not to lose her composure.

"I'm so sorry…" I inclined my head toward her brother, who was standing a short distance away under a tree with Chief Andrews next to him. "How is Tony holding up?"

She shook her head. "He's devastated, and not being able to go talk to her family made it even worse at the funeral. I'm hoping we can talk to them here, if Max hasn't poisoned them against us," she said, shooting a dark look toward Max.

"I'm not sure I understand why he's so hostile," I said. "I mean, did he know that Tony had been pursuing her again?"

"Unfortunately, yes, he did. He saw them together about a week before she died and went ballistic! He threatened Tony and told him he better stay away from her or else." She shook her head.

"Or else what?" I asked.

She shrugged. "Natalie pulled him away before he could elaborate."

The graveside service started, so we ended our conversation. I moved to stand by Lisa, and Frankie joined her brother.

As I looked around at the crowd, I was surprised to see Tom standing about ten yards away. He wasn't close enough for me to see his expression, but he seemed to be focused on what was going on at the funeral. I wondered what he was doing here...

Chapter Seventeen

fter the graveside service, we'd decided to get something to eat at Frankie's. I'd wanted to talk to Tony, but I'd seen that he and Frankie were hanging back, obviously hoping to speak to Natalie's parents, so I'd decided then wasn't the best time. I'd wondered if the restaurant would be open since I'd seen almost all their staff at the funeral, but apparently, some of them had skipped the graveside service to open the diner, anticipating lots of people wanting to grab a bite to eat before heading back to work.

The place was packed, but we found a four-top in the back corner. Kristi hurried up with drinks for all of us and apologized that it would be a bit before she could take our order. After she rushed away, I saw Tom come through the door and look around for an empty table.

Lisa saw where my attention was and asked me, "Who is that?"

"Tom," I answered nonchalantly, but something in my demeanor must have given me away, because she suddenly waved him over to our table.

"Would you like to join us?" she asked. "This place is really full, and we have an open chair. I'm Lisa, by the way, and you know my husband, Mike, and my best friend, Ellen."

I shot daggers at her as Tom took the chair beside me.

"It's nice to meet you, Lisa," he said to her and nodded at Mike. Then he turned to me. "How are you holding up? The funeral must have brought back some bad memories for you." He sounded sincerely concerned.

"It was hard," I acknowledged. "Especially during Tara's eulogy. I was surprised to see you at the graveside. I didn't realize you knew Natalie. You didn't mention that before." I looked directly at him to gauge his reaction to my statement.

His eyes got big for a moment before he seemed to relax and answered, "I didn't really know Natalie, but I'd met her a few times and found her to be a bright and beautiful person. I'm really sorry she's dead." There was a measure of guilt in his voice that I didn't really understand, but I didn't get a chance to pursue it, as Lisa started interrogating him.

"So, where are you from? And how long have you been in town?" she asked without giving him a chance to answer before continuing. "Are you married? What do you do?"

Mike interrupted her to address Tom. "Sorry about that. She gets a little carried away sometimes."

We all laughed, including Lisa.

"It's okay. I know in small towns, everyone knows everyone and everything about them, so I'm a novelty around here." Tom smiled. "I guess that's the good thing and the bad thing about being in a small town. Everyone knows all your secrets, and you stand out if you're a stranger."

He continued after a moment, looking thoughtful. "I've lived all over the country as part of my job. I just got to town about a month ago, but I'm considering making the move permanent. I really like it here and have enjoyed getting to know some of the people." He shot me a look that made my face heat, and of course, Lisa noticed.

"Oh really," she said, her eyes lighting up with mischief. "You know, Ellen is staying with us while her car is in the shop. Maybe you could come for dinner one night."

As he started to nod in acceptance, I spoke up. "I'm sure Tom is really busy, and besides, my car should be fixed tomorrow."

"Then let's make it tonight," she said. "Does that work for you, Tom?"

He accepted quickly, not giving me a chance to derail this obvious attempt at matchmaking by my best friend. We would have words about this later.

Several people stopped by our table to chat while we were eating. As was to be expected, everyone wanted to talk about either the murder or the funeral, or both. I told the story of finding the body over and over again till I was ready to hide out in the back room if one more person asked me about it. Lisa noticed I was getting antsy and started redirecting people's conversations before they could ask me about it. Although one of her conversational gambits was to introduce Tom, so I wasn't sure if he appreciated her efforts as much as I did. He was beginning to get a deer in the headlights look by the time the fourth or fifth group came to the table.

I whispered, "The problem with sitting with us is that one or more of us knows pretty much everyone in the room, so if you wanted a peaceful lunch, you probably should have waited for a bar stool."

I smiled to let him know that I was teasing, and he laughed, which lit up his face. It made his eyes sparkle and made his already attractive face irresistible. I stared for a minute too long before I realized what I was doing and turned back to my food.

We were just getting ready to leave when Frankie walked in with Tony. I popped up from the table and hurried over to them. I squeezed Frankie's hand and then impulsively hugged Tony. "I'm so sorry, Tony," I said. "I can't imagine how hard this is for you."

He thanked me, and then he looked over my shoulder, and his eyes narrowed. "What is he doing here?"

I turned around and tried to see who he was looking at. I realized Tom was in the direct line of sight. "Do you mean Tom?" I asked.

"Is that his name?" he said. "He's the big bad fed that promised Natalie she would be safe if she talked to him, and now look at her." He started toward Tom, but by then Tom had paid and slipped out the door.

"What does Tom have to do with Natalie?" I asked, but Frankie had already pulled Tony into the back room to calm him down, and I was left with more questions than answers. He had told me he worked in cybercrime, so what did that have to do with Natalie and/or Max? Maybe I wouldn't kill Lisa for inviting him to dinner if it gave me a chance to get some answers.

Every time I thought I was starting to know what was going on, I got a piece that seemed to be from an entirely different puzzle than the one I thought I was trying to put together. I was beginning to think this was more like the 1,000-piece puzzle of a baby seal on snow that Noelle had given me one Christmas. The shades of white were so subtle, it was nearly impossible to solve.

Chapter Eighteen

hile I helped Lisa make dinner, I thought about everything I wanted to ask Tom when I saw him. How did he know Natalie? What did Tony mean about him talking to Natalie? Did he know what was on the flash drive, and did he have it? If not, why did Max think he did?

The real question, though, was how I was going to get him to talk to me, since every time I started asking him questions, he clammed up. After our lunch together, I felt like he was more approachable, but I wasn't sure it was enough for him to answer my questions.

Lisa had made her best "company" dinner of roast beef, carrots, potatoes, green beans, fried apples, and rolls. The house smelled amazing! I knew how good a cook Lisa was, so I was really looking forward to it. Tom arrived right on time, and we settled around the table. The food was excellent, and besides complimenting Lisa on it, Tom was quiet for the first part of the meal. He gradually relaxed and joined in the dinner conversation so well, it felt like we had known him all our lives. The conversation flowed effortlessly from subject to subject, with none of those awkward lulls that sometimes happen when a group of people who know each other so well they can talk in shorthand try to include someone new.

As we finished eating, Louisa started whining. "I think I'm going to take her for a walk so I can work off some of this wonderful meal before we have dessert. Anyone want to come?" My glance included everyone at the table, but I was really hoping Tom would take me up on it.

Lisa begged off, and before Mike could say anything, she told him he needed to help her in the kitchen.

He shrugged and told Tom, "You should go. We can handle it. We'll have dessert when you guys get back."

Lisa winked at me when I went into the kitchen to grab Lou's leash. "Have fun!" she trilled, clearly proud of herself.

I rolled my eyes and then went back out to find Louisa and Tom.

We set off at a brisk pace with Louisa sniffing at all the yards as we walked toward downtown Cascade through a neighborhood of large old homes with wonderful porches.

I smiled wistfully. "I've always wanted a wraparound porch with rockers and porch swings. They always look so inviting, like you want to curl up on the swing and read a book or just people-watch. I love to people-watch."

Tom smiled. "Yes, I've noticed how much you see that others don't pay attention to."

I wasn't sure what to make of that comment, and neither of us spoke again until we had gone through downtown and turned toward the park entrance.

He reached out and touched my arm to get my attention. "Why don't we sit for a minute?" He gestured to a nearby bench, and I sat and tied Lou's leash to the arm so she could still wander a bit without taking off. He settled next to me and turned toward me with a serious look on his face but didn't say anything for a while.

The silence grew uncomfortable, but I decided I shouldn't try to fill it and waited as patiently as I could for him to speak.

"I owe you an apology," he finally said, and I raised my eyebrows in question. "I was very abrupt with you when we were talking at your house." He stopped again and nervously ran his fingers through his hair. "It's been a long time since I met someone I like." He took my hand. "And I've lost the cadence of a conversation you have when you're getting to know someone." He absently rubbed my hand.

It felt wonderful, and I could feel myself leaning towards him, but it also distracted me, and I couldn't afford to be distracted. I extracted my hand, leaned back, and started petting Louisa. She sat down next to me and leaned against my leg. "I think if I got the chance to know you, I would like you too, but every time I ask you about yourself, you turn cold. Why?"

He dropped his head for a moment, but then he looked back up at me. "I can't tell you everything, at least not yet, but as I told you the other day, I work on a federal task force investigating cybercrimes. Specifically, I work for the U.S. Secret Service Cyber Fraud Task Force. I came to town to follow a lead in an investigation I'm trying to wrap up. This is my last case. I'm ready for a change, and I really like it here in Cascade." He shot me a look that made me melt.

"So how is Natalie's death connected?" I asked, hoping he would at least tell me something, but he shook his head.

"I can't talk about my investigation, and I don't know if Natalie's death had anything to do with it or not." He seemed sincere. "The police chief seems to think it was more of a domestic thing."

"Is that why you were in there talking to Chief Andrews the day I came by the station?"

He nodded. "The chief is aware of my investigation. But it's you I'm worried about." He took my hand again and looked into my eyes. "If the crime I'm investigating *is* involved, you're in incredible danger, and I don't want anything to happen to you. Can't you leave this to the police? *Please?*"

I sighed. "I really didn't intend to investigate. I just thought I'd talk to a few people and try to understand what happened to Natalie. If that helped Tony, that would be a bonus. But then someone left the message on my car. At first, I was terrified, and I wanted to hide out. But between the nightmares and the fear, I decided I would have no peace until whoever did this was put behind bars. I'm trying to be careful, but I need this resolved."

"But why can't you let the police handle it?" he asked.

"Because they seem to be looking in the wrong direction," I said sadly. "But I promise I'll let Chief Andrews know everything I find. And I'll be careful." That was as much as I could promise right now. I wanted my life back. I didn't want to be afraid all the time. I squeezed his hand and gave him a half-smile.

"I guess I'll have to be satisfied with that for now. I want the chance to get to know you, Ellen, when there doesn't have to be secrets between us."

He leaned toward me, and my pulse quickened. I thought he was about to kiss me, but then his eyes went wide at something behind me. He suddenly pushed me to the ground and covered my body with his as shots rang out from somewhere behind me. The streetlight above us exploded, and broken glass rained down on us from above. I heard Tom grunt, and then tires squealed as whoever shot at us sped off.

Chapter Nineteen

"A re you okay?" Tom asked as he gingerly rolled off me. Without even letting me answer, he had his phone out, dialing 911. "Shots fired downtown near the park entrance. It was a black SUV, but that's all I saw."

The concrete below me felt cold against my skin. I was struggling to catch my breath after having it knocked out of me by the impact.

Just as Tom started to hang up, I felt something sticky and wet under my hand and realized there was blood pouring out of Tom's arm.

Before he could hang up, I yelled, "Send an ambulance!" I hoped they'd heard me before he hung up, but from the sirens in the distance, I knew help would be here soon. "You're hurt!" I sat up and tried to reach for his arm, but he stopped me.

"It's just a cut from the glass. I'm not sure they even shot directly at us. If they had, I don't know how they could have missed." He ripped off a piece of his T-shirt and wrapped it around his arm.

Suddenly, I heard whining. In all the chaos, I had forgotten about Louisa. "Oh my gosh! Louisa!" I scrambled to where she was tied. While the bench had protected her a little, she was covered in cuts. Some were shallow, but several seemed to be pretty deep and were clearly painful. I pulled her onto my lap and held her, but I had nothing to use to stem the bleeding. I felt Tom behind me. He pressed more of his T-shirt into my hand. I glanced around and gave him a worried smile as I applied pressure to the worst of Louisa's cuts.

Chief Andrews hurried up as an ambulance arrived behind him. "We put up roadblocks as fast as we could and asked for assistance from the state police, but nothing yet."

Lisa and Mike came running up. "We heard the call on the scanner," Mike said. "Are you okay? What happened?"

"Someone shot at us," I said hurriedly, "but I'm fine. It's Tom and Louisa who need help!"

Tom tried to shrug off the EMTs, but the chief pushed him down onto the bench. "Let them take a look at you. We don't need you bleeding out because you're too stubborn."

Mike looked at Louisa for a moment and started running toward his house, calling over his shoulder, "I'll get the car. Lisa, call the emergency vet. I'll be back as fast as I can."

Lisa pulled out her phone and stepped away as I continued to cradle Lou in my arms. I felt strangely calm as I pressed the shirt against her side. It was soaked with blood, but the chief walked up with some gauze pads and elastic bandages he must have gotten from the EMTs when he escorted Tom over to them.

He took the T-shirt from me and replaced it with a gauze pad as he tore off a strip of bandage to hold it in place. "When

Mike gets back, you head to the vet," he said gently. "Can I ask you some questions while you wait?"

"Sure," I agreed. "Is Tom okay?"

"He'll be fine. It wasn't a bad cut. Just bled a lot. They'll give him a couple of stitches." He indicated the EMTs. "Can you tell me about what happened?"

"I don't really know," I said slowly. "We were sitting on the bench, talking." I blushed, thinking about the almost kiss. "Then Tom must have seen something, because he pushed me to the ground just before two shots rang out. The light exploded and poured glass down on us. I didn't see anything because I was facing the wrong way, and then Tom was covering me. I heard a car speeding away, but that's all. It happened so fast. I'm sorry!" I had started to shake all over, and someone draped a blanket around me.

"Don't worry about it." He dismissed my apology. "Ellen, I'm concerned." He placed a hand on my shoulder. "While Tom doesn't think the shots were aimed at you, it's clearly an escalation. I'm going to have a patrol car follow you to the vet and stay to escort you back to the Partridges'. I know Mike has a state-of-the-art security system, so I think you'll be okay there, but please don't go anywhere alone until we figure out what's going on here."

I nodded but thought, *How long can I stay cooped up?*

Just then, Mike honked his horn to alert us that he had arrived. The chief bent down and picked up Louisa for me. As I started to get up, I felt strong arms pulling me to my feet. I turned to find Tom staring at me. "I need to get Louisa to the vet. Are you sure you're okay?"

He smiled. "I'm fine. I wish I could go with you, but I need to help the chief figure out who that could have been."

I kissed his cheek and paused before getting into the car. "Thanks for protecting me tonight." I dove quickly into the car, not giving him a chance to respond.

Mike sped off, and I leaned down to cradle my dog.

We didn't return home until nearly three a.m. The vet had to keep Louisa. She'd lost so much blood that they had to give her a blood transfusion, and she had more stitches than I could count. They wanted to keep her as calm and quiet as possible so she didn't break open any of her wounds. I was bereft. I was so used to having her with me that I wasn't sure I'd be able to sleep.

I took a quick shower to wash off the blood that was all over me. I wasn't sure if it was Tom's or Louisa's, but it was probably some of both. Despite the hot shower, I was freezing as the events of the night had finally caught up with me.

Lisa came in to check on me just as I slid under the covers. "Are you okay?" She sat next to me on the bed and hugged me for a long time.

"I'm not sure." I started tearing up. "I feel so horrible that Tom and Louisa got hurt because of me."

"Not because of you," she insisted. "It's whoever the evil person is who killed Natalie."

"But if I wasn't asking questions, no one would have shot at us."

"You must be closer to figuring it out than you think, or no one would have taken a shot at you." She yawned hugely, and I shooed her off to bed.

As I lay down, I couldn't help but wonder if she was right. The problem was I had no idea which questions had elicited this response. I finally allowed all the emotions I had been bottling up for hours to bubble up to the surface, and I cried myself to sleep.

Chapter Twenty

woke to the smell of bacon, but when I tried to move to get up, I fell back on the pillows and groaned. I hurt in places I didn't even know could hurt. I looked in the mirror to see red and swollen eyes from last night's crying jag. Farther down, one whole side of my body was covered in bruises, from my shoulder to my knee. I guessed that must have been where I landed when Tom pushed me down. I slowly dressed in leggings and a soft sweatshirt but skipped socks, as moving my arm and leg on that side really hurt. Then, I phoned the vet to check on Louisa before limping down the stairs for breakfast.

I was surprised to see not just Lisa and Mike, but Tom sitting at the kitchen table.

He stood when I walked into the room. "I needed to see how you were doing. Pretty sore, from the way you're walking." He winced. "I'm sorry I couldn't cushion your fall."

"Nonsense." I walked over and sat down. "You were protecting me. How are you?" I frowned at the bandages covering his left forearm.

"It's not bad," he said, resuming his seat as Lisa set a mug of hot chocolate in front of me. "It'll probably itch some as it heals, but it doesn't hurt too badly at the moment."

Lisa placed a plate filled with bacon, eggs, and sourdough toast in front of me. "Have you talked to the vet yet this morning? How's Louisa?" she asked as she joined us at the table.

"I talked to them just now. The doctor said she needs to remain calm and quiet at least today to let the wounds scab over and begin healing before she starts moving around too much. I can go see her around dinnertime if I want, but he said it would be better if I waited until tomorrow, because she might get too excited." I moaned. "My poor sweet puppy girl! I hate that she got hurt because of me."

Three sets of eyes glared at me, so before they could say anything, I held up my hands in surrender. "Okay, not *because* of me, but you have to admit if I hadn't been poking around asking questions, no one would have shot at me."

"How do you know it was you they were shooting at?" Tom asked quietly.

My eyes shot up, and I stared at him, unblinking, for a minute. "You think that was meant for you?"

"Maybe," he said slowly. "We're both 'poking around,' as you said, in things other people don't want us to, so it could just as easily have been me who was the target."

"So maybe you both need to be really careful until whoever is responsible is caught," Mike said with steel in his tone that brooked no argument.

I smiled sadly at him. "I won't be doing anything today except lying on the couch." My smile turned into a mischievous grin as I felt my spirits lift a bit with the support of my friends. "I'm too sore and tired to cause trouble today."

"I have to head to the office for a few hours," Lisa interjected, "but Mike will be just around the corner at the garage if you need something." She gave me a quick hug and headed upstairs to finish getting ready.

"Do you want me to stay with you?" Mike asked. "If you don't feel safe here alone, I can get someone to cover for me." He looked me directly in the eye to make sure I knew how sincere he was.

"That's okay." I smiled at him. "I'm going to binge-watch something on TV and rest."

Mike left through the back door after reminding me to set the alarm when Lisa and Tom left.

"I assume you need to leave, too." I looked at Tom, who had started to fidget a bit, like he was late for something but felt guilty about leaving. "Before you do, can I ask you something?"

"Sure," he said, "and I'll answer if I can."

"That's fair," I acknowledged. "Do you know anything about a flash drive that Natalie might have had of Max's?" I was watching him carefully, or I might have missed the tightening of his jaw. He instantly relaxed it.

"I don't know anything about it." He seemed sincere, but I knew what I'd seen. If he didn't know about the flash drive itself, he knew why she might have had it.

"Okay." I feigned indifference. "I just thought you might know if one was found with her body."

He shook his head and then stood up. "I'm sorry to leave you, but I need to get to work too." He took my hand. "I'm glad you weren't hurt any worse last night. Please be careful today, okay?" He squeezed my hand briefly and then left, leaving me wondering what I was going to do about the mysterious Mr. Green.

Chapter Twenty-One

I planned to have a lazy day, trying to heal up from last night's events, but before I could relax, I was going to need to call Noelle. I was actually surprised I hadn't heard from her yet. As fast as gossip flew through this town, I had expected a call first thing this morning. Even though she had moved thirty minutes away, she normally knew everything going on, sometimes before I did. I settled onto the couch in the living room and dialed her number.

"Hi, honey! Before I say anything else, I'm okay and safe."

"Why wouldn't you be okay and safe?!" she asked, sounding alarmed.

"Um. Well, something happened last night." I struggled to figure out how to tell her this gently. "Uh, Tom and I went for a walk after dinner, and someone took a shot at us."

Before I could continue, she interrupted, "*Took a shot at you!* What do you mean, someone shot at you?! Where did this happen? Did they arrest whoever did this? Is Tom okay? Why did you go for a walk?" She was asking questions so fast that I couldn't get a word in edgewise.

She finally wound down, and I jumped in before she could work herself up again. "We are both fine," I hurried to reassure her. "Tom and Louisa both have some cuts from the light that was shot out, but they are both recovering. I just have a few bruises where Tom pushed me to the ground."

"I'm coming over right now!" she practically yelled into the phone.

"No, you are not!" I said, using my best "Mom" voice. "You have classes this morning, and I am perfectly fine. I'm locked in at Lisa's with the alarm set. I'm not going anywhere today, so you don't have to worry about me. Go to class, and then we'll talk."

"I'm coming over as soon as I finish my seminar," she insisted, and this time I acquiesced.

"Okay, honey, I'll see you later this afternoon." We said goodbye, and I could feel tears welling up in my eyes. I had come so close to making her an orphan last night. It was still hard to believe that someone had actually shot at me. I was just a small-town girl, not someone people deliberately shot at! And I did think it was me they were shooting at, despite Tom's attempt to deflect.

Just after noon, Noelle came to check on me and brought me lunch. When I let her in, she started to hug me really tight, but I gasped in pain.

"Oh, Mom, you are hurt!"

"I'm just bruised up. Nothing serious," I reassured her.

"What were you thinking, being outside in the open like that? You knew someone had threatened you!" she scolded, and once again, I felt like she was the parent and I was the child.

"I had Tom and Louisa with me, so it never occurred to me it would be unsafe." I started to tear up, and so did she.

She gave me another hug, gentler this time. "I'm so glad you are okay! I don't know what I would have done without you."

We sat and ate the burgers and fries she had brought and didn't talk much. It was enough just to be together. I convinced her that I would be fine if she went to her art class in the afternoon, and she left reluctantly, with plans to come for dinner the next night.

I kept turning everything over and over in my mind, but the pieces didn't fit together, and I eventually fell asleep in front of the TV, too tired from my short night to stay awake. When I woke up, there was a true crime show on, and it didn't take long before I was completely engrossed in it.

It involved cryptocurrency, which caught my attention since I had just talked about it with Mike a few days ago. In the show, a lawyer was mixing his clients' funds with those from criminal operations to "launder" the money through crypto transactions. The announcer discussed cryptocurrency mixers as services that obscure cryptocurrency transactions. They combined funds from multiple users and then redistributed them, making it difficult to trace the flow of specific funds on the blockchain. None of his regular clients had any idea that he was using their funds, and neither did the authorities until a disgruntled ex-girlfriend of the attorney blew the whistle on him.

The amount of money involved was staggering! Hundreds of millions of dollars had been laundered.

I told Lisa and Mike about it over dinner. Lisa had picked up Mexican food from my favorite restaurant on her way home, as the previous short night had made us all too tired to mess with cooking.

Lisa took a sip of her drink. "That makes me think of that show on Netflix. What was it called?" she asked Mike.

"*Ozark*, I think, or something like that."

"That's it. There was a financial planner who was laundering money for some drug cartel. When something went wrong, they moved to the Ozarks to get away. We watched a few episodes."

"Hmm," I hummed. "Maybe I'll have to check that out. I wonder if that's the kind of thing Tom investigates?"

"Speaking of Tom..." She smiled. "What's going on there? You two seemed pretty chummy this morning."

"I don't know!" I groused. "Sometimes I think he really likes me, but he has so many secrets, it's hard to feel like I know enough to really be able to tell what he thinks. Maybe when all of this is over, we can see what happens."

"For what it's worth, I think he's a stand-up guy," Mike interjected.

I was surprised. "What makes you say that?" I asked curiously. I valued Mike's opinion all the more since he rarely gave it.

"His first thought last night, when the bullets started flying, was protecting you. That makes him the kind of man I would want to share a beer or a foxhole with." He grinned sheepishly as Lisa and I both stared at him open-mouthed. That was high praise indeed.

That night, I had a terrible dream. I was back on the trail in the park, walking Louisa, and I found Natalie's body again. Only this time, I felt this horrible dread before suddenly bullets started flying all around me. I had to dive under the tree limb for protection, only to find Tom lying there bleeding from a gunshot wound. I surged up with a cry to discover it was still the middle of the night. It felt so real, I was shaking. I was afraid to go back to sleep, lest I go right back into the nightmare, so I pulled on a robe and went down to the kitchen to get a glass of water.

Suddenly, the motion sensor lights came on, lighting up the backyard like a football field on Friday night. I saw movement in the back corner of the yard near the gate to the alley that ran behind the house. Mike came barreling down the stairs with a handgun.

"Go up to the master bedroom and lock both you and Lisa in," he said urgently. "Stay away from the windows!" He slipped out the door, staying in the shadows at the edge of the lawn.

I ran up the stairs, heart in my throat, and found Lisa sitting up in bed, yawning.

"What's going on?" she asked sleepily as I turned the lock on the bedroom door.

"Someone's in the backyard," I said, pulling her down behind the bed. "Mike went out to investigate and told me to lock us in up here."

"Mike went out there alone?" She shot up, and it took all my strength to pull her back down. She dove for her phone on the nightstand and started dialing 911.

Focusing on keeping Lisa safe kept me from succumbing to the fear coursing through me.

Just then, there was a pounding on the door. "It's me, Mike," he said forcefully. "It's all clear. You can open the door."

Lisa threw her phone onto the bed and jumped up to open the door. As he stepped into the room, she launched herself into his arms and began scolding him. "What were you thinking, going out there alone?"

"Shh! It's okay," he soothed, holding her close and rubbing circles on her back until she relaxed.

I felt just a twinge of jealousy, wishing I had someone to hold and reassure me. It had been a rough twenty-four hours, and I felt like I was hanging on by a thread.

Mike continued, "I was pretty sure they had already left when the lights came on. I just wanted to see if I could see how they got in and what direction they went."

"And did you find out?" I asked, feeling the adrenaline still surging through me.

"They broke the lock on the gate, but they were long gone by the time I got there." He had on what I called his soldier face—his jaw so tight it could cut glass and his eyes icy. He was clearly unhappy he hadn't seen where they went. "I called Chief Andrews, and he's on his way over. We're going to check the cameras when he gets here. You may want to get dressed, Ellen. I'm sure he'll want to talk to you."

As I hurried to my room to change, I wondered if I would ever have a good night's sleep again.

Chapter Twenty-Two

They didn't find anything very helpful on the cameras. The person was dressed all in black and had a balaclava covering most of his face. We hadn't gone back to bed until nearly six a.m., but even then, none of us could sleep. Lisa went in to work, and I was nursing a hot chocolate at the kitchen table, watching Mike fix the lock on the back gate. He was planning to install some additional cameras back there as well.

I couldn't help but feel guilty. My being here had put my friends at risk. If anything had happened to Mike last night, I would never have forgiven myself. My car should be done today. I wondered if I should plan to go home. The thought of being out at my house alone terrified me, but putting my friends in more danger was worse. I felt tears well up in my eyes. What was I going to do?

Just then, my phone rang. I was surprised to see it was Tara. "Hi, Tara."

"Hi, Ellen. I hope this isn't a bad time to call."

"No," I said while thinking it could have been better.

"I was wondering..." She hesitated. "Look, I could really use some help at the store today, and I thought, well, if you were serious about maybe wanting to be a partner with me, this might be a good time to try it and see if you enjoy it," she finished quickly, as if hoping to sweep me along with her.

"Um..." I thought before continuing. "How long would you need me, and when?"

"Could you be here by noon? I would need you until about four," she promptly answered. "That's when the high school girls come in, and I'll be back to close. I thought I could work with you for the first hour and show you the ropes before I have to leave for an appointment."

"Okay," I said decisively. Maybe this was the distraction I needed, and I wouldn't be sitting around, worrying about what to do. "I'll be there by noon. Thanks for thinking of me, Tara!"

"Thank you for pitching in." She sounded relieved.

I rushed upstairs to take a shower and change into something "boutique" appropriate. I had a cute denim trouser skirt that came about mid-calf that I paired with gray ankle boots and a soft gray, red, and black argyle sweater I had bought at Someone Else's Closet a few months ago. A little blush and concealer for my dark circles, and I looked as good as I could after too many nights with little to no restful sleep. By the time I was ready, Mike had finished putting in the extra security.

"What are you all dressed up for?" he asked, taking in my change from the sweats I'd had on when he went outside.

"Tara called and asked me to help out in the store for a few hours. I should be done by four. Do you think you could take me to get my car then?"

"I'd be glad to, but do you think it's safe to be going out?" he asked doubtfully.

"I'm sure it will be okay." I tried to sound more confident than I actually felt. Inside, I was quivering with both excitement and fear. "I'll be in a public place surrounded by shoppers. You know what Friday afternoons are like in town. I doubt I'll ever be alone."

"Why don't I at least give you a lift over there? I have to run to the shop anyway, and then I'll have my car for when I pick you up to go get yours from the tire place." He still looked unsure about me going, but I was sure he knew I was going a little stir crazy, so he didn't say anything more.

I readily agreed, and we headed out. When I arrived, the store was packed with shoppers, and I dove right in to help them find the items they were looking for. It wasn't until we had a lull that Tara could show me how to use the register.

"I'm sure glad you got here when you did," she exclaimed. "I've been overrun this morning with customers. Fridays are normally steady but not as busy as today has been. I hate that I have to leave you alone so soon, but I couldn't put off this appointment any longer. I have to meet with the insurance people about Natalie's life insurance. We each had a policy on the other so that in the event something happened to either of us, we wouldn't lose the business. With the shop being closed for several days, we really need that influx of cash to keep us afloat."

"Is that a typical thing for small businesses?" I asked curiously.

"It was something the lawyer who drew up our partnership agreement suggested. He indicated it was the best way to protect the business from something unforeseen." She sighed. "I thought we might need it if one of us got sick or in an accident. I never dreamed one of us would be murdered." She shuddered.

"I've always worked in a government or corporate environment, and I wasn't aware that was a thing, but I'm sure glad you have it to fall back on under the circumstances," I said sympathetically.

"Do you feel comfortable with the register now?" She slipped on her jacket and grabbed her purse.

"I'll be fine," I said. "You go do what you need to do, and don't worry. I'll hold the fort."

There was a steady stream of customers for the first couple of hours, and I found I really enjoyed chatting with them and helping guide them to clothing or accessories that were flattering. I really might like joining Tara as a partner.

There was another lull, so I began straightening up, rehanging clothes from the fitting room, and picking up items that had fallen off their hangers. Once I finished that, I started straightening the checkout desk area. I saw something sticking out from under the desk, but before I could try to retrieve it, the bell rang, indicating I had a new customer.

I looked up to see Max Holland striding toward me. He looked like a man on a mission, but he tried to cover his agitation with a charming smile that didn't quite reach his eyes. I felt myself straightening up and trying to project competence. "I met you at the funeral, didn't I? I didn't realize you worked here." He reached out to shake my hand but only grasped my fingers and quickly released them and stepped back a step. If I didn't know better, I would think I was the one intimidating him.

"Ellen Douglas, and I don't work here normally. Tara just needed someone to fill in while she had an appointment."

"Ah, that explains it. Do you know when she'll be back? I really need to talk to her about something."

"She said she would be back to help close but didn't tell me a specific time. Sorry," I said with a small frown, showing I wished I had better news for him. "Is there anything I can help you with?"

"Tara didn't mention whether she had found anything of mine, did she?" he asked hopefully.

I shook my head. "Sorry, no. We really didn't have a chance to talk because it was so busy."

Just then, several shoppers entered the store.

Max looked annoyed at the interruption. "I guess I'll have to come back later. If you speak to Tara, will you let her know I'm coming?"

I nodded but was already moving to help the customers as he turned and left.

It was busy until just before I was due to be relieved. I finally bent down to try to pull out whatever was under the counter. It was a piece of computer paper with a bunch of words that didn't make sense. "Clutch, pigeon, brother, lava, fox, symptom, rhythm, cradle, timber, sword, noodle, eagle," I read aloud, trying to make sense of this random set of words. What on earth? Could it be a code of some kind? I took a quick picture of it with my phone, and then I decided to stick the paper in the back of the notebook Tara used to record the various sales for those who consigned their clothes to the store. It would be easy for her to find it in case it was something important. I'd have to remember to tell her about it when I talked to her next.

I had just finished giving the girls a message for Tara, letting her know Max would be stopping by, when Mike came to pick me up. My phone rang as I got into the car. It was the vet letting me know Louisa was ready to come home now. I assured them I would be there as soon as I got my car. I couldn't wait to be mobile and have my beloved companion back with me.

Chapter Twenty-Three

It felt so good to have my car back and even better to have Louisa. Poor girl had to wear a cone to keep her from licking her wounds, but she was wagging her tail like mad when I walked into the exam room at the vet's office. She was still pretty loopy, but the doctor said she should be more alert tomorrow. The meds he was sending home with me would help keep her calm, too, since she was going to be pretty sore, and I knew from experience that she would fight the cone. On more than one occasion in the past, she had managed to get it off over her head. I would have to keep a close eye on her.

We headed back to Mike and Lisa's. Mike had told me if I insisted on going home, he and Lisa would be going with me, and since their house had much better security than mine, I decided to stay at their house for now. I still felt guilty about putting them in danger, but it did make me feel warm inside that they cared so much about me. I was blessed with good friends.

Lisa, Mike, and Noelle were all there when Louisa and I went inside. Noelle immediately began making a fuss over her while shooting me daggers with her eyes. "Why didn't you tell me someone tried to get in here last night?"

I frowned at Lisa, but she pointed at Mike.

"I thought she should know so she can be careful too, just in case." He shrugged.

It hadn't even occurred to me that Noelle could be in danger or that someone might hurt her to get to me. I suddenly felt sick to my stomach and grabbed the chair in front of me.

"Don't freak out!" Noelle put her arm around me. "I'm fine. Mike and Lisa invited me to stay here for a few days with you, but I'm actually going out of town for that internship interview in Louisville. I'll head out as soon as we finish dinner, and I'm meeting some friends in Madison for the weekend, so you don't need to worry." Her face changed as she thought for a minute. "Unless you need me to stay here, Mom? I don't have to go—or, better yet, you could go with me and get out of here for a while." She looked at me hopefully, and I gave her a side hug.

"I need to be here to look after Louisa, and she's in no condition to travel. She would be miserable in a car for hours." I smiled gently at her. "But thank you for asking me. You go and have a good time with your friends. I'll feel a lot better if at least one of us is out of harm's way." I encompassed Lisa and Mike in my look.

"Don't worry, Noelle," Lisa added. "We'll keep an eye on your mom. Now, let's eat."

Just as we sat down at the table, the doorbell rang. Mike went to answer it, and we heard male voices coming toward the dining room. Mike reentered the room with both Tom and Chief Andrews.

Lisa jumped up. "Why don't you both join us for dinner? We have plenty." Before they could even respond, she had two more place settings at the table and was offering them something to drink.

The chief started to beg off, but when he saw the pulled pork on the platter, he changed his mind. "I do love smoked meat, so I guess it wouldn't hurt to take a minute to eat if you're sure you have plenty." After Lisa assured him that we had more than enough, he went to the other room to call in and let the office know where he would be for the next few minutes.

Tom slid into the seat next to me. "How are you doing? Sorry I didn't get back to check on you last night."

"I'm doing okay. I actually ended up going to fill in at Someone Else's Closet today," I said, smiling.

As we started passing around the pulled pork, baked beans, and mac and cheese, Lisa piped up. "I was surprised when Mike told me you had done that. I didn't know you were interested in retail."

"It was a bit of a surprise to me, too. The other day, I ran into Tara outside her house, and she was saying she might need a partner. I've been looking for something I could do, so I told her I might be interested. Today she needed someone to fill in, and I thought it would be a good chance to see if I liked it."

"And did you?" asked Noelle.

"I did like it," I said after considering the question for a moment. "I didn't expect to enjoy it as much as I did. It was fun helping women find things that made them feel good about how they looked. I was only there for a few hours, though, so I'm not sure it's a big enough sample to know for sure that I would like it long term."

The conversation moved on to other topics, and it was a very nice, relaxed meal. Both Tom and Chief Andrews—"Call me Jim"—were great at telling stories. We lingered over dessert, laughing and talking, until Noelle said she needed to get on the road.

I offered to walk her out, and Tom insisted on going with us, reminding me that I couldn't just go about my business as usual. I hugged Noelle goodbye and watched out the front door until I saw her car pull away. Then Tom took my hand and pulled me over into the formal living room.

"Can we talk for a minute before we join the others?"

"Of course," I responded, curious about what was on his mind.

"I heard about the intruder last night. I talked to Mike earlier, and he agreed that an extra guard would be good, so I'm going to stay on the couch downstairs tonight." He looked at me, gauging my reaction to his news.

I frowned. "Is that really necessary? I mean, Mike's security system worked last night, and the person didn't get anywhere near the house. You were hurt the other night, and I bet you aren't 100 percent yet. I doubt sleeping on the couch will do your wounds any good." A part of me felt safer knowing he would be there, but another part was frustrated that no one had talked to me before deciding what was going to happen.

"I'm sorry if this upsets you," Tom said, squeezing my hand, "but I'll be fine on the couch, and I really want to help make sure you're okay. I thought Mike might sleep easier, too."

"Okay," I said, resigned. It would be better for Lisa's peace of mind, as I knew last night had been really hard on her. "We'd better go join them. I suspect the chief didn't come by just to have dinner."

Tom nodded, and we went into the family room to find Mike, Lisa, and Chief Andrews deep in conversation.

They looked up when we came in, and the chief looked at us seriously. "I really have to get back to the office, but I was just telling the Partridges that we haven't found anything definitive about who the intruder was last night. We did catch a glimpse of a black SUV on a couple of doorbell cameras from the neighbors. It appeared to be similar to the one Tom described when you were shot at, but that doesn't really mean anything, since half the people in the area drive a black SUV."

"Do we know if any of the suspects drives one?" Tom asked hopefully.

"None of them drives a black SUV. Tony has a pickup truck. Max drives a BMW, and Tara has a Prius."

I was surprised that the chief was being so forthcoming. Maybe having dinner together made him feel more comfortable sharing.

"What I don't understand," I said, puzzled, "is why they're still trying to get to me. I haven't even asked anyone a question since the shooting incident. And my only interaction with the 'suspects' was Tara teaching me to run the register and Max coming in to see her. He didn't even stay, just said he'd be back, and he didn't return while I was there."

"Could be they think you saw something or know something you aren't aware of," Tom suggested.

"Or they think you have something they want. Any idea what that could be?" the chief asked me.

I thought for a moment. "The only thing I know that's missing is the flash drive that Max was looking for at The Grounds the other day, but I've never seen it. He was looking for something today at the shop, too, but it was something he thought Tara might have seen. I assumed it was the flash drive."

"This is the first I'm hearing about a flash drive," the chief said, giving me a stern look.

I gave him a sheepish look. "A lot has happened in the last few days, and it slipped my mind." I filled him in on what I had heard at The Grounds.

"I assume from your response that you didn't find one on Natalie's body, so I wonder what happened to it." I turned to Tom. "I know you can't tell us much about your investigation, but any idea what might be on that flash drive?"

"I can't say much, but it's possible that Natalie may have stumbled upon something in Max's files that someone doesn't want to get into the wrong hands." Tom was visibly uncomfortable even saying that much, so I didn't press for more information.

The chief excused himself to go back to the station, and the rest of us settled around the game table to play a board game. Mike and Lisa had a bunch of games, and we found that Tom already knew how to play most of them. We settled on Ticket to Ride, as I wasn't sure I could focus enough on any of the more complicated games. I was happy to think about something other than the danger I was in.

During the game, we talked about our families. I found out Tom was divorced and had a daughter in Missouri who was in her mid-twenties. Mike and Lisa told Tom they were both previously divorced and had four grown children and three grandchildren between them. We spent most of the game talking about how hard it was to know how to parent adults. I confessed I was looking forward to grandchildren, and Tom surprised me by saying how much he was looking forward to them too.

He turned out to be just as competitive as Mike and beat all of us soundly, but we had fun. I was excited to find some things we had in common and was hoping we would get a chance to explore that more once all this was over. He took Louisa out for me for the last time before bed.

I stopped to tell him to be careful before heading up.

He smiled. "Don't worry. I'll be fine. You get some rest. I've got your back." He gave me a quick hug that left me feeling warm and protected as I headed upstairs.

Chapter Twenty-Four

woke up early the next morning, feeling rested for the first time in a long time. No nightmares and no night visitors were a refreshing change. I spent a little extra time getting ready, picking out some leggings and a cute tunic with pockets. I even put on a little bit of makeup. I told myself it was because I didn't know what I might do that day and that it had nothing to do with Tom being downstairs. I was hoping his night had been just as uneventful as mine.

He was already at the table drinking some coffee when I got to the kitchen. Louisa was resting her head on his foot, which pushed her cone up against his leg. It looked very uncomfortable, but when I started to make her move, he stopped me.

"It's okay. She's been hanging out with me all night. She's been out this morning, but I didn't know what to feed her."

"I hope she didn't keep you up." I moved to the fridge to get her food, and she jumped up as soon as she heard the door open.

"No, she was fine. She curled up right next to the couch on the rug. It actually helped me get more rest than I expected, since I knew she would hear anyone coming way before I would."

Louisa went back over to him and put her head on his knee. He scratched behind her ears.

"You keep doing that, and she'll probably adopt you," I laughed. "So, I take it we didn't have any intruders last night?"

He shook his head. "No sign of anyone. I'll check the camera feeds with Mike when he comes down, but I didn't see anything, and Louisa didn't alert at any point. How did you sleep? Any nightmares?"

"I slept great," I said cheerfully. "No nightmares for the first time since I found Natalie. I can't tell you how much better I feel after a full night's rest."

"I bet," he said with a smile.

Just then, Mike and Lisa came in, and the men went off to check the cameras while Lisa and I started making breakfast. Soon, the kitchen was filled with the smell of sausage and biscuits, and I had started making the gravy while Lisa scrambled some eggs.

"It was sweet of Tom to stay last night to protect you." Lisa smiled knowingly at me. "I think he really likes you. And I think you like him at least a little, or you wouldn't have put in so much effort getting ready this morning." She gestured to my outfit.

I squirmed under her scrutiny but didn't get the chance to respond, as Tom and Mike came back in to eat.

"See anything?" I asked, hoping my change of subject would deter Lisa from pursuing the earlier topic. She smirked at me but didn't say anything else.

"No sign of anyone in the yard or around the house," Mike said, "but there was a car parked in the alley all night. It was too far down to get much of an idea of what it was, but it was dark and looked like an SUV. I'm going to call Chief Andrews after breakfast and let him know."

"Were you planning to go anywhere today, Ellen?" Tom asked. "If you can avoid it, it might be safer to stay in."

"I was going to see my mother, but I guess I can put that off another day," I said reluctantly. The thought of being cooped up again made me antsy, but I didn't want to be an easy target either.

Just after they all left, the phone rang.

"Hello, Ellen? It's Tara."

"Hi, Tara. Hope everything worked out with the insurance people yesterday."

"It did. Thanks for asking. I should get a check for the in-surance within the week. That is really going to help give me some breathing room until I can find a new partner. Which actually leads me to why I called. What did you think yester-day? Did you enjoy being at the shop?" She sounded hopeful, and while I didn't want to discourage her, I wasn't quite ready to commit.

"I did enjoy myself," I told her honestly, "but I think I would probably want to spend some more time in the shop before I would want to start talking about a commitment. What would you think about letting me work there some for the next few weeks so I can figure out if that's where I want to put my energies going forward?"

"That's a great idea," she enthused. "I don't want you to commit unless it's really what you want, and that would give us a chance to work together more, too. See if we have compatible working styles. Why don't you send me the hours you'll be available next week, and I'll add you to the sched-ule."

"Sounds good to me. By the way, did Max come back in to talk to you yesterday? He said something about you finding something of his," I said, hoping she would assuage my cu-riosity.

"Oh, yes, he came in at closing. Unfortunately, I had no idea what he was talking about," she sighed. "He was very unhappy about that, but finding a piece of paper when he won't even tell me what's on it is like looking for a needle in a haystack."

"Speaking of pieces of paper... When I was straightening up behind the counter, I noticed a piece of paper sticking out from under the desk. I pulled it out, and it was covered with random words, like *timber* and *sword*. I thought it might be a code of some kind, so I put it in the back of the consignment book." I hoped Tara would take the hint that maybe the paper was the one Max was looking for, and she didn't disappoint.

"I have no idea what that was." She paused, as if she were thinking. "You don't suppose that was the paper Max was looking for, do you? I mean, if anyone would use a code, wouldn't it be a lawyer?" She chuckled. "I certainly can never figure them out. I'll mention it to him if he calls again."

We signed off with me promising to send her my availability to work the next week.

Could she be right about the paper belonging to Max? If so, what was it doing under the desk at the shop?

I decided to see if I could figure out what the words might mean. It was probably an exercise in futility since I knew nothing about codes, but I decided to see if Google could help.

I started with the first letters of each word, but there was only one vowel, so unless it was some Slavic or Scandinavian name with too many consonants and not enough vowels, that wasn't it.

I looked up the most common types of codes using words. If it was a code where one word represented another word, I'd never figure that out without the key. I decided to try two types that sounded like I might be able to figure them out. The first was a substitution cipher, where each letter represented another letter. I spent quite a bit of time counting letters and trying to see if I could figure out the most common—Thank you, *Wheel of Fortune*, for letting us know the most used letters. No luck with that one.

Then I tried a transposition cipher, which the internet said meant rearranging the letters or words. Rearranging the words didn't seem to do anything since they didn't seem to be related to each other at all. I then tried to rearrange the letters, but since I really had no idea what I was doing, I got nowhere. I finally got so frustrated that I decided to take a break and have some lunch.

Just as I was starting to make a sandwich, Mike came in. "Hey, I thought maybe you'd like some company for lunch."

He smiled. "I know it's hard feeling cooped up, but I really do think it's safer for you."

I gave him a half-smile. "I know. Doesn't mean I have to like it, but I know it's the wisest thing to do. Thanks for coming to keep me company. I've had a frustrating morning. Can I make you a sandwich? There's ham, roast beef, or turkey."

"Sure. Surprise me." Mike smiled and grabbed the chips and some drinks while I finished the sandwiches, so we continued the conversation at the bar.

Mike took a bite of his sandwich and smiled at me. "Great sandwich."

I had given him ham and turkey with two kinds of cheese, lettuce, and tomato on sourdough. I just had ham and cheddar. I smiled back, glad to have accomplished something this morning.

"What was so frustrating this morning?"

I explained about finding the paper at Someone Else's Closet and my conversation with Tara about it, which made me think the paper might belong to Max. "I tried seeing if the first letters would spell something out and then working out substitution and transposition ciphers. No luck at all." I shook my head. "I'm no closer to figuring out why this is important now than I was when I started."

"Do you mind if I look at it?" Mike asked curiously. "I had a little experience with codes when I was in the military. Maybe something will ring a bell."

I texted him a copy of the picture I took.

He looked at it and frowned. "There's something about this that rings a bell, but I can't quite bring it to mind. Let me ponder it this afternoon while I'm working. Maybe if I stop trying to think of it, it'll come to me."

He headed back to the office, and I let Louisa out in the backyard to play for a bit.

I decided to bake something for dessert for tonight's dinner. Lisa had put some chicken in the slow cooker, and I wanted to feel like I was contributing. I made a Dutch apple pie and had just put it in the oven when my phone rang. It was Mike.

"Hey, Ellen, I had a thought." He sounded as excited as he ever did. "Remember me telling you about that class on cryptocurrency that Max taught?"

"Yes."

"Well, one of the things he talked about was seed phrases, which are essentially passwords to access your cryptocurrency accounts. He said one of the safest ways to keep track of them was to use a paper wallet, which is a piece of paper with your seed phrase printed on it."

"Okaaaaay," I said, still having no idea what he was getting at.

"Well, the paper you sent me has twelve words on it. That's a typical size for a seed phrase, and they're often made up of random words so no one can guess them. Do you think this could be Max's seed phrase for his crypto wallet?" He sounded uncertain, almost as if he couldn't believe that could be the answer.

"It's certainly a possibility, but what on earth would it have been doing under the counter at Someone Else's Closet?"

He chuckled, and I could almost hear him shrugging. "No idea. I consider myself lucky that I might have figured out what the words are to begin with."

Laughing, I thanked him, and we hung up.

I sank down into a nearby chair, trying to think through what this could mean. What did I know?

1. Max is looking for a missing flash drive.

2. Max thinks something of his is at Someone Else's Closet.

3. I found a paper that may be Max's cryptocurrency seed phrase.

Now for conjecture. Could the seed phrase have been with the flash drive? If so, what could be on that flash drive? And why would Natalie have had it? Could Max be involved in something shady, and Natalie took the flash drive as proof? Did she know she had the seed phrase for the account? I felt like some of the puzzle pieces were getting closer to fitting together. But how did I fill in the missing pieces?

Chapter Twenty-Five

I really needed to see my mom, but I had promised I wouldn't leave the house, so I asked Lisa if she could bring her home with her so she could have dinner with us. They arrived just as my pie came out of the oven.

"Ellen!" my mother cried as she pulled me into a tight hug. "I have been worried sick about you." Today, she was in skinny burgundy pants with a matching long cardigan over a patterned blouse with her signature pearls. I felt distinctly underdressed even in my leggings and tunic, especially since Lisa was still in her office clothes.

"I'm fine, Mom! Honestly! Mike and Lisa are keeping me safe here. They have top-of-the-line security." I helped her sit and moved her cane out of the way so Lisa and I could finish making dinner.

"I heard that new guy was over here helping protect you, too. What is going on there?" She gave me a pointed look that said she wasn't happy that I hadn't been keeping her informed.

"Where did you hear that? And his name is Tom," I said, exasperated. I didn't want to have this conversation with my mother. "Have you heard anything else about the murder?" I asked, hoping to change the subject.

She frowned, recognizing that I was deflecting, but apparently, she was too excited to share what she'd learned, so she let me get by with it. "I've heard a couple of things."

Lisa and I exchanged amused glances. How she heard everything in the retirement home, I would never know.

"We were playing cards again the other day, and I heard that Natalie was stabbed with something of an unusual shape."

"What kind of shape?" I asked, remembering the conversation I overheard the chief having in his office about Natalie being stabbed.

"Well, my friend's grandson works for the coroner's office, and he told her it was triangular-shaped." She gave me a self-satisfied look that showed she knew she was giving me valuable information.

"Why would your friend's grandson tell her that?" I asked, flabbergasted that someone would tell their grandmother this kind of detail about a murder.

"Well, he didn't actually tell her exactly," she hedged.

"Then how did she find out?" I asked suspiciously.

"We've been talking a lot about the murder at meals. Everyone has a theory about who is responsible, so we decided to start a betting pool about it. Nancy, my friend, waited until her grandson came to visit after work and then sent him out to the courtyard to check on her hanging plants. While he was outside, she snooped in his backpack and read some of the reports."

"Please tell me you are not gambling about Natalie's death!" I practically shouted, and she had the grace to look ashamed. "That is awful!"

"I guess it is, but we just get so bored that we have to have something to do." She gave me the pitiful look she used when she was trying to make me feel guilty.

It didn't work this time. "I don't care how bored you are. That is completely inappropriate!"

Lisa stepped in. "So, who do you all think did it?"

My mom seemed relieved to move on from my scolding. "It's evenly divided between Max, Tony, Tara, and some madman who randomly killed her."

My curiosity overcame my disgust at their pool. "Did she find out anything else? Like what kind of weapon would cause a triangular wound?"

"Well, nothing else from Nancy, but Tony and Frankie's great-aunt said that Natalie told Tony that Max was not the man she thought he was, and she was trying to figure out what to do about it." She said it matter-of-factly, like she had clues in murder investigations every day. But I guess to be fair, she had found out way more than I had.

"Did Natalie tell him what Max had done to cause her to feel that way?"

She shook her head.

I decided to change the subject, and we had a nice visit through dinner. Mike drove her back after dinner, and Lisa and I took our drinks into the family room.

"What do you make of all this, Ellen?" She looked at me pointedly.

"I don't know what to think." I shrugged. "It feels like I have a puzzle with most of the pieces, but I can't figure out how they fit together. I thought I was on to something this afternoon, but I'm just not sure." I sighed. "I want this to be over. I want my life back."

She squeezed my arm. "While I love having you here, I understand why you want to get back to your life."

We settled in to watch a movie once Mike got back and were just about ready to turn in when the doorbell rang. Mike went to answer it while I finished eating my pie, and he returned with Tom.

I looked at him, surprised. I didn't expect him to come back tonight.

He smiled at me. "Is that apple pie? I could sure go for a piece."

Lisa hopped up before I could. "Do you want it warm with ice cream?"

"That would be great!" He smiled at her.

"I didn't expect you back tonight, Tom. After all, nothing happened last night," I told him.

"Doesn't pay to become complacent," he said, reaching down to pet Louisa. "She looks better than she did even this morning."

I smiled. "She's definitely feeling a little better. I had to wrestle the cone back on her twice."

Tom leaned down and gently rubbed her neck under the edges of the cone. "Yeah, I bet this thing isn't very comfortable, huh, girl?"

Lou shook her head right at that moment, as if answering him, before looking up at him pitifully.

We were laughing when Lisa came back in with a bowl of pie and ice cream.

Tom took a large bite and closed his eyes, groaning as he chewed. Once he'd swallowed, he said, "This is excellent, Lisa."

"Wish I could take credit for it, but Ellen made it this afternoon." She smiled, and then she and Mike excused themselves to go upstairs to bed.

I started to follow, but Tom grabbed my hand before I could go. "Stay and talk to me a bit..." He gave me his most charming smile, and I melted a little as I sat back down. "How was your day?"

"It was pretty uneventful since I couldn't leave the house." I smiled wryly. "How about you? Have you been working ever since you left this morning?"

"Pretty much. But it's been a frustrating day. I came up with lots of questions but very few answers." He yawned hugely, and I stood.

"I think you need some sleep. Maybe tomorrow we can compare notes. I have a feeling that if we put our heads together, we might find some answers."

I headed up to bed, a little excited that we'd have time together in the morning to talk about everything we had learned. Even if he couldn't be completely open with me, I hoped it would be productive for us both. And to be honest, I had enjoyed the time we had spent together the last few days. It felt like we were getting past the awkwardness that had characterized our first few interactions. I fell asleep smiling with anticipation.

Chapter Twenty-Six

When I walked into the kitchen for breakfast the next morning, only Lisa and Mike were sitting at the table. "Where's Tom?" I had expected him to be drinking coffee again when I came down.

"He was already gone when we got down here." Mike sounded disgruntled. "I wish he would have told me he was leaving so I could have kept watch."

"Did he leave a note or anything?" It seemed odd that he would leave without telling any of us. I had built up our planned talk this morning so much in my mind that I felt like crying in disappointment when I found out Tom was gone.

"He left a note saying he had an emergency at work." Lisa handed me the note.

Ellen, Mike, and Lisa —

I had an emergency at work and had to leave unexpectedly. Sorry, I couldn't stay the whole night. Since I didn't want to wake anyone up at that hour, I asked a patrol car to keep an eye on things. I don't know how long I'll need to be gone to address this issue, but I'll check in when I can.

Tom

So, he wasn't just gone this morning, but potentially for several days. I was going to have to put aside my feelings and get on with it. I really felt like he had some of the pieces I needed to finally put this puzzle together, but I guess I'd just have to keep digging on my own.

Mike asked about my plans for the day, and just as I was about to answer, my phone rang. It was Tara asking me if I would like to work today. I jumped at the chance since I was so tired of being cooped up. I also thought it would keep me from thinking too much about why Tom had left so suddenly.

Mike said he would drive me, and I hurried upstairs to get ready. When I got back down, I heard Mike on the phone.

"She'll be working all day at Someone Else's Closet. Uh-huh. That's right. I'll drop her off and pick her up. Thanks." He hung up the phone.

"Who was that?" I asked, wondering why he'd called to tell someone where I would be.

"Chief Andrews. I thought since he wanted you to stay here, I should let him know that you were going to be out today. He thinks it'll be okay since you'll be right downtown, but if anything suspicious happens, please call one of us and we'll be right there." He locked his gaze on me until I nodded in agreement.

When I got to the store, it was really busy again, so I didn't get a chance to ask Tara if she had told Max about the paper I stuck in the ledger until a few hours later. "Hey, did you ever figure out if the paper I found was what Max was looking for?"

"Now that was a strange conversation..." She shook her head. "He just gets weirder and weirder every time I talk to him."

"How do you mean?"

"Max used to be the epitome of a successful lawyer. Always cool, calm, and collected. Frankly, that's part of why I never really took to him. He's always been cold and given off the vibe that he's better than everyone else, but I put up with him because Natalie seemed to really care about him."

I nodded at her, hoping she would continue.

"But about a month ago, he started acting really possessive of her. He'd come in, he said, to 'see her,' but I thought it was really to check up on her."

"Do you think that was because of Tony trying to win her back?" I asked.

"It could have been, but when it first started, Natalie still wasn't giving Tony the time of day, so I'm not sure that was it. Although I don't think that helped. Frankly, I was getting concerned about Natalie, too, as she started to be secretive. She would leave unexpectedly from the store for an hour or so at a time in that last week before she died and never tell me where she was going."

"I take it that was unusual for her?" I tried to plug that into the information I already had.

"Very unusual. She normally told me everything. But things really came to a head when Max came by the day before she died, and I saw him grab her wrist really hard and yank her out the back door. When she came back inside, she was rubbing her wrist."

"I'm sure that would make me really worried too," I said encouragingly.

She continued, seeming to need to get the whole story out. "The next morning, I caught her in the alley behind the store with Tony. That's what precipitated the fight we had. I told her I was worried that Max was hurting her and that seeing Tony was only going to put her more at risk. She got really defensive and then stormed out." Tara wiped tears from her eyes, and I gave her a hug.

"I'm sure she knew you were just concerned about her. It's a best friend's job to be honest and tell us the things we need to hear, whether we want to hear them or not," I said, hoping to comfort her, and she smiled a sad smile.

"Anyway..." She shook herself, like she was shaking off the bad feelings. "You asked about Max and the note you found. When I told him about it on the phone, he sounded really paranoid and asked who else had seen it. I told him only you and I, and he insisted I put it in the safe until he comes to get it. He's supposed to come later today."

I mulled that over. I was surprised he hadn't come to get it right away if our theory was correct, and it was his cryptocurrency seed phrase. I decided to see if Tara knew anything about that.

"Mike was telling me about Max giving a seminar about small businesses using cryptocurrency."

She nodded. "He kept trying to get Natalie and me to sign up for it. In fact, I think I may still have a card he left here once with a QR code on it to access his crypto website." She started rummaging through a drawer and handed me a credit card–sized paper with a QR code next to a picture of Max and his law firm's address and information. "You can keep that if you're interested in it. It always seemed like too much trouble to me."

"Thanks, Tara. I may check it out."

Just then, some customers came in, and we got busy helping them.

At lunchtime, Chief Andrews popped in with paninis from The Grounds.

"Let me guess," I said, laughing. "My daughter told you what I like."

"I plead the Fifth," he said, pulling out sandwiches and drinks for all three of us. "Just wanted to check in and make sure there had been no other incidents."

"Incidents?" Tara asked, and I had to explain about the shooting and the intruder.

"Oh my gosh, Ellen! That's awful! Why would someone do that?" She seemed sincerely upset for me.

The chief answered for me. "We don't know for sure, but the working theory is that Ellen either knows something she is unaware of or they think she knows something. Either way, we are trying to make sure she is safe."

"And I appreciate that," I interjected. "Nothing else has happened, and I haven't had that sense that someone is watching me, like I did in the park a few days ago."

"That's good," he said, taking a big bite of his sandwich. "I'm still going to have patrols going by here and the Partridge house frequently just in case."

He stood up to leave, and I reached out and squeezed his arm. "Thank you for looking out for me and for bringing lunch."

"Anytime." He smiled and took his leave, promising a patrol car would be by later.

We got busy again right after he left, so Tara and I didn't have a chance to talk anymore for several hours. Time flew by until it was almost time for me to leave. In walked Max, looking even more harried than he had the last time I saw him. The man was unraveling, and I saw no sign of the cool, calm, and collected lawyer Tara had described. His eyes were bloodshot, and he had dark circles under them, as if he hadn't been sleeping. His tie was askew and his shirt wrinkled. He looked like he had been sleeping in his clothes and had a pronounced five o'clock shadow.

He walked up to the counter and addressed Tara harshly. "Did you put it in the safe as I asked you to?" He didn't even acknowledge that I was there at all.

Tara jumped back a bit at the tone and then stiffened her spine and looked him directly in the eye. "Yes, it's in the safe. I put it in an envelope with your name on it." She turned to the little safe behind the counter and started inputting the combination. She was careful that neither Max nor I could see the numbers she put in. She quickly removed an envelope and handed it to him.

He pulled out a letter opener from his suit jacket's inside pocket and slit open the envelope. He pulled out the paper, took a quick look, and visibly relaxed. Then he turned his gaze to me. "Tara said you found this. Did you show it to anyone?"

"No." I shook my head. Of course, I didn't mention I'd taken a picture of it...or shown it to Mike. "I just put it in Tara's consignment book and let her know it was there." I hoped I didn't sound as nervous as I was feeling with him glaring at me the way he was.

"Good." He reached to put the letter opener back in his pocket, and I realized it was a replica of a sword in miniature. It was about ten inches long and looked exactly like the ones I'd seen in historical movies on TV. Without thinking, I blurted out, "Is that a sword?"

He stopped putting it away and pulled it back out. "It's a replica of a short sword carried by my ancestors back in medieval times." He held it out proudly, and I saw it had a sheath covering the blade, which explained how he could carry it in his suit safely. "Natalie bought it for me last Christmas. I carry it with me everywhere now as a reminder of her." For a moment, I saw a grief-stricken fiancé instead of the angry menace he'd been acting like the other times I'd seen him, and I wondered if I had misjudged him. Maybe he was just overcome with grief and angry that his fiancé had been murdered. I would be angry if I lost someone like that.

"It's beautiful!" I admired it. "It looks so real." I almost reached for it, but something held me back.

Abruptly, he shoved it into his pocket, and the mask of anger came back onto his face. "I have to go." With that, he turned and hurried out without a backward glance.

"Whew," I said, turning to Tara. "The anger in him is palpable!"

She moaned. "I'm just glad it's done with. Hopefully, he'll have no reason to drop in on us again."

I silently agreed with her.

Just before I left, Tara pulled me aside. "You will be careful, Ellen, won't you?" she asked, her voice shaking a bit. "I know you haven't agreed to be my partner yet, but I have really enjoyed working with you the last few days, and I don't think I could handle it if something happened to you, too."

"I promise, Tara, I'm being really careful," I assured her. "And I have really enjoyed the last few days too. I'm excited to work with you more next week."

She gave me a quick hug before I grabbed my coat and hurried out to meet Mike.

Chapter Twenty-Seven

ike dropped me off and then returned to work. I found Louisa snoozing on the rug in front of the couch. I was pleased to see that she still had her cone on, since my biggest fear in going to work was that she would find a way to get it off and then rip open her stitches. I took her out back and let her run around a bit. She seemed much more energetic than she'd been yesterday, so I hoped that meant she was healing well.

When we got back inside, I plopped down on the couch, weary and a little discouraged. It didn't feel like I was any closer to narrowing down exactly what had happened to Natalie, and until I did, I couldn't go home and get my life back. Or could I? Maybe I should think about putting in security at my house so I could go home. I loved my friends, but I was tired of living out of a suitcase. I wanted to sleep in my own bed and soak in my own bathtub. I wanted Louisa to have her yard back. I made a mental note to ask Mike when he got home about what kind of security he would recommend I get and how much it would cost to install it.

I wondered if Tom would be back this evening. I really wanted to have that talk we were supposed to have this morning. It might help clarify several things for me, and he might have some good ideas about security, too.

As I let my mind drift a bit, I realized that I still hadn't had a conversation with Tony. I'd spoken at length with Tara and talked to Max a bit—and to others around Max a bunch too—but I had only briefly spoken to Tony. Everything I knew about him had come from other people. I wondered if I went to Frankie's for lunch tomorrow, whether I might run into him. I was going to try it anyway.

I started thinking about what questions I wanted to ask him:

1. Do you know what Natalie found out about Max that made her want to break off her engagement?

2. What did you mean about Tom promising to protect Natalie?

3. What did you talk about in the alley with Natalie the morning she was killed?

4. What time did she leave you, and do you know where she planned to go?

5. Did she ever mention a flash drive? If so, what was on it, and where do you think it could be?

My phone buzzed as I was finishing my list, and when I reached into my pocket to get it, a card fell out and dropped onto the floor. I ignored it for the moment and answered the phone.

"Hello," I answered without looking to see who it might be, slightly distracted by the card I had dropped.

A familiar baritone voice came over the line. "Ellen, this is Tom. Sorry about this morning. I wanted to let you know I'm going to be gone for a couple of days, following up on something."

"I understand that you have to do what your job demands, but I was really hoping for that talk we were going to have this morning." I tried not to sound as disappointed as I felt.

"I'm sorry I had to leave so suddenly. This was an urgent situation, and I had to leave around three a.m. I didn't want to wake you up since I know you haven't been sleeping well," he said apologetically.

"That's okay. I hope it means that you're close to wrapping up your case." I was trying to be encouraging.

"I hope so too. It's looking promising." He sounded both hopeful and exhausted. "I promise I'll be back as soon as I can, and we'll talk. If everything goes well, I may be able to speak more freely when I get back than I can now."

"Please take care of yourself and be careful."

I was concerned after we hung up. He sounded so tired, and I knew his arm still wasn't healed.

I had way too many feelings surrounding him, and I wasn't sure what to do with them, so I decided to focus instead on the card that fell out of my pocket when he called. This was the first time I'd had a chance to examine it since Tara gave it to me. It was one of those glossy plastic cards that felt almost like a rewards card from the supermarket.

On the front was Max's picture with his phone number and email, as well as his law firm's name and address. Then on the back was a QR code with a note that read, *For crypto transactions, please use this QR code.*

I decided to use my phone to scan the QR code and see where it would take me. It came up with a menu that had two choices. The first was to initiate a cryptocurrency transfer. The second was to authenticate.

I picked the second option, and it came up with a request for the private key. Could Mike be right that those random words on the paper I found were Max's private key? I decided that before I tried anything with them, I should do some research. If I had Max's private key and I authenticated, would he be able to tell that I had accessed the account?

At this point, I didn't even know if this was related to Natalie's death, but my gut said it was. I wished Tom were back, because I thought he would be able to advise me on what to do with all this.

About that time, Lisa came in from work, and I went to help her make dinner. Maybe Tom would wrap things up and come back tomorrow. If he didn't, I'd have to think about taking this to Chief Andrews.

Chapter Twenty-Eight

fter an okay night's sleep—I only had the nightmare once—I called and spent the morning talking with a security system installation company Mike had recommended over dinner the night before. They wanted to meet me at my house to do a full assessment before they could give me a complete estimate, but they couldn't come out till tomorrow. I was disappointed, but at least I was moving toward getting some of my life back. I sent Mike a text asking if he would be able to go with me the next day to meet with them, and he said yes. *Yay*! One thing off my to-do list.

By the time I was done with that and paying some bills, it was nearly lunchtime, so I decided to head to Frankie's to see if I could get a chance to talk to Tony. I stuck my list of questions in my pocket, but I doubted I would need to refer to them. I had been pondering them over and over in my mind all night.

When I walked in, it felt a bit like coming home. I was normally here several times a week, and the only time I had been here in the last week was after the funeral. Kristi came up and gave me a hug when I walked in, and then Maria brought me a Coke Zero as I slipped onto my usual stool at the counter.

"How are you, Ellen?" she asked. "We've missed you hanging out here."

"It's been a little crazy," I answered with a wobbly smile. "A lot has happened in the last few days."

"I heard you got shot at!" Kristi said with an incredulous voice.

"Well, shots were fired *near* me, at least," I answered wryly, thinking of Tom's theory that they only intended to scare us. "I'm fine, but Louisa got cut up pretty badly."

Everyone around the counter expressed their concern for Lou, and then we settled down to general chit-chat. These were people I had eaten lunch with for months, and we knew enough about each other to keep up a constant flow of conversation.

I had just gotten my food when Frankie came out of her office and sat down next to me. I leaned over. "How are you doing, Frankie?"

She shrugged. "Hanging in there."

"How is Tony holding up?"

"He's struggling," she said, looking sad. "I really think he was in love with Natalie, and he's going to be grieving for a while."

I hesitated before asking my next question but decided to go ahead and ask. The worst that could happen was she could say no. "Do you think he would be up to talking to me? I have several questions that I think he could shed some light on."

Frankie started shaking her head. "Ellen, you need to let this alone. I know I said I wanted you to help clear his name, but I had no idea how dangerous that would be. First, your car was attacked, and then you got shot at. I would never forgive myself if you were hurt trying to clear my brother."

"It's too late to back off now." I touched her arm. "I want my simple life back, and as long as the killer is out there free, I'm not going to be safe. I stopped asking questions for a few days, and someone still tried to break into Lisa's, so I need to solve this if I want my life back." I glanced around and lowered my voice. "I think I'm close, but I have some holes I think Tony can help fill in. Can you at least ask him if he'll talk to me?"

She didn't look happy, but as she got up from her stool, she agreed. "I actually expect him to stop by in about half an hour. If you can hang out, I'll let him know you want to talk to him."

I smiled. "I guess that's the excuse I need to have some pie."

She gave me a strained smile and headed back to her office.

I lingered over my cherry pie and continued to chit-chat until Tony walked in. He saw me and gestured toward a table in the back. I grabbed my drink and my bill and headed over to join him at the table. The dark circles under his eyes showed he hadn't been sleeping, and my heart went out to him.

I waited till he'd ordered, and then I dived in. "I know this may be difficult for you to talk about, but I'm trying to figure out what happened to Natalie. I don't know if Frankie told you, but someone has been trying to warn me off asking questions. They slashed my tires, shot at me, and tried to break into my friend's house, where I'm staying."

The more I talked, the wider his eyes got until he started shaking his head. "I had no idea... That is crazy!"

"I'm sure you can understand why I want to figure out who is behind all this." I smiled a bit weakly. "I'm hoping you can help me do that."

"I'm not sure I know anything for sure that can help, but I'll give it a shot." He straightened up in his chair as if bracing himself for a blow.

I decided to limit my questions to only the most essential. "Do you know what Natalie found out about Max that caused her to decide to break off her engagement?"

"No." He shook his head. "I only know she overheard him talking on the phone to someone, and it made her suspicious. I begged her to tell me more details, but she didn't want to involve me."

"What did you mean when you said Tom had promised to protect her?"

Tony's face instantly turned red, and he took a deep breath and visibly tried to calm down. He exhaled and started talking rapidly. "I saw her with him at the coffee shop and asked her who he was. I admit I was jealous. At that point, she had said she was breaking up with Max, but she hadn't agreed to come back to me yet. I thought maybe he was a rival, so I confronted her about it. She said she was meeting with him to tell him about something Max was doing, and she was going to give him evidence that would result in Max's arrest. She thought that would make her safe. Why didn't he protect her?" He teared up, and I reached out and patted his hand.

"I don't know what happened exactly, Tony, but Tom seems to be a good man, and I don't think he would have left her unprotected if he'd known she was in imminent danger." I knew he might not want to hear that from me, but I felt the need to defend Tom.

I could tell he wasn't happy with my response, and I was afraid he was going to cut me off, so I quickly asked one more question. "I understand that you met with Natalie in the alley behind Someone Else's Closet the morning she died. Do you know where she was planning to go when you finished your conversation?"

He reluctantly answered, "I don't know for sure. She mentioned needing to meet someone at the park later, but I'm not sure if she was going somewhere else before the park or not."

I stood and thanked him, knowing I had all the answers I was going to get from him today. I paid my bill and went back to Lisa's to think.

Chapter Twenty-Nine

fter I got back to Lisa's house, I went out into the backyard with Louisa and threw a ball for her. She wasn't quite back up to par but was definitely feeling a lot better than she had a couple of days ago. As usual, when she brought me back the ball, she wouldn't release it, and I had to pull it out of her mouth so I could throw it again. We had been playing for a while when I noticed that instead of coming back to me, she was staring at the back gate intently and emitting a low growling sound.

I didn't want to take any chances, so I called her to come and hurried into the house, locking the door behind me and arming the alarm. I quickly called the number on the card Chief Andrews had given me. "I think there may be someone outside the back gate," I told him when he answered, and then I explained Louisa's behavior.

"I have someone nearby. I'll have them swing by. Why don't you call and let Mike know, too? I'd rather you weren't there alone." He paused thoughtfully. "Is there a landline you can use to call Mike so you don't have to hang up with me?"

"No, they just use their cell phones." I was trying not to freak out, but I'd started to shake, and Lou came over and pressed against me, whining.

"Then let me have someone here call him. I'd like you to stay on with me until my deputy checks out the alley and Mike gets there." His voice was calm and soothing, and I'd started to relax a little when I heard a bang out back and jumped up startled by the noise. The alarm began blaring.

I ran to the window, which I knew in the back of my mind was a terrible idea, but I had to know what was going on. The gate was open and banged again when it swung back against the latch.

In the backyard was a man dressed all in black, staring at the back of the house. He yelled, "You need to stop asking questions, or the next time, I won't miss."

He lifted his finger like it was a gun, pointed it at me, and pretended to pull the trigger. Then he turned and ran out through the gate. I could hear him laughing loudly as he ran.

"Ellen! Ellen, can you hear me?"

I realized the chief had been frantically trying to get my attention, and I finally responded.

"Someone was out in the backyard. He told me to stop asking questions, pretended to shoot me, and then ran away laughing." My voice was small and emotionless. I felt numbness spreading throughout my body. They always seemed to know where I was and when I was vulnerable. I walked over to the panel, pushed the buttons to shut off the blaring of the alarm, and then quickly rearmed it in case the man came back. The silence was almost worse. I could feel my heart pounding.

"I'm coming right over, and Mike should be there any minute. He can remotely access the alarm to get in, so why don't you just relax until we get there?" He was trying to soothe me again, but this time I was too numb to appreciate it.

Mike came rushing in and found me on the floor beneath the alarm panel, leaning against the wall with my arms wrapped around Louisa. I was shaking so badly, he had to help me stand, and then he guided me to the couch and wrapped a blanket around me. "Just sit. You're safe now. I'm here, and the chief will be here any moment."

By the time the chief arrived, Lisa had come home too and was sitting beside me on the couch, rubbing my arm. The shaking had started to subside, but I still felt a bit detached, like I was watching what was happening in the room from far away. Chief Andrews and Mike went to Mike's security room to review the camera footage while Lisa tried to distract me.

"Are you hungry?" she asked gently. "I could fix you something."

I shook my head. Food did *not* sound good at the moment. "You don't need to do that for me, but if you're hungry, go ahead. I'm sure Mike will be when he's done with the chief."

"Maybe I'll order a pizza, and it'll be here when anyone wants to eat."

I nodded at her, but I couldn't imagine being hungry anytime soon.

She'd just finished placing the order when Chief Andrews and Mike came back into the room.

"Do you feel up to talking now?" The chief sat in the recliner across from me.

"Sure," I said, not really sure I was telling the truth. What I really wanted to do was run and hide under the covers till the boogeyman was gone.

"Take me through your day," he started.

I told him about talking to the security system company and then going to Frankie's for lunch.

"So, lots of people knew you were out around lunch?"

I considered for a moment. "It wasn't super crowded in there today, and I think I recognized everyone, but someone could have seen me going in and leaving."

He nodded. "Did you talk to anyone specifically when you were in there?"

I squirmed a little. He wasn't going to like my answer. "Obviously, Frankie and the usual counter folks. And Tony." I tried to say it like it was no big deal, but I saw the skin around his eyes tighten, and his mouth pulled down in a frown.

"Ellen," he barked, but Mike put a hand up to stop him. He gave him his military stare, and the chief took a deep breath before continuing. "Anyone else?" he practically growled out.

I shook my head.

"Did you see anyone on the way home or notice if you were being followed?"

Again, I shook my head. "I was pretty deep in thought, so I wasn't really paying enough attention, I guess," I said, embarrassed at my lack of self-preservation instincts. I might as well have been the dumb person in a slasher flick who goes in the open door of the haunted house. "I feel so stupid that I didn't think to check for a tail."

"It probably didn't matter," he reassured me. "They already knew where you are staying since we had the incident the other night."

"So, you think it was the same guy?" I asked.

Mike interjected. "From what we saw on the camera, he had the same build and a similar disguise, so it was probably the same guy. Not being able to see his face makes it tough to say for sure, but my gut says it was the same person."

The chief said, "I agree."

Before he could continue, the doorbell rang, and Lisa went to get the pizza.

Surprisingly, I was hungry, and we retired to the dining room and talked about other things over dinner. I was quiet, thinking things through in my mind while they chatted. I thought it was time I told someone everything I knew or had guessed. When we finished the meal, I stood. "If you can stay, Chief Andrews, I'd like to tell you everything I've learned."

We all settled down in the living room. Lisa made sure everyone had something to drink before I started to talk.

"I want my life back, so I've been trying to figure out what happened. I have a lot of puzzle pieces, and I think a picture is emerging, but I'm still missing some key pieces. I'm hoping that by sharing what I know and what I suspect, maybe it will give you some pieces that you don't have that may help solve this, so I can go home." I felt myself tearing up.

"I can't really share anything about an active investigation, but I would like to hear what you have to say, even though I thought you were going to leave the investigating to my department." He gave me a wry smile, and I returned it with a sheepish one of my own.

Lisa jumped to my defense. "People who might not talk to you will talk to her."

The chief nodded in acknowledgment. "That's true, but it's also why we had the incident today, so the price of those conversations may be too high."

It was my turn to acknowledge his point. "That's true, but the threats began before I'd even really started asking questions, so I'm not sure it's my investigating that's causing the issue. When the threat was put on my car, I'd hardly even talked to anyone, so it makes me think the threats started because of my finding the body, more so than any questions I asked."

The chief made a noncommittal gesture but indicated I should continue.

"What I believe happened is that Natalie discovered something about Max that made her decide to break her engagement. Whatever she found may have been on a thumb drive, because Max has been desperately looking for one he said was lost. I think it may have something to do with cryptocurrency, because I found what I believe to be the private key to his crypto wallet at Someone Else's Closet, hidden under the desk. It also seems Natalie may have been informing on Max to Tom, or at least planning to, as she told Tony she was going to meet someone the morning she was killed to turn over evidence. Tom is out of pocket, so I haven't been able to ask him about that yet. Do you know, Chief?"

He shrugged. "I guess I'm not giving anything away by confirming that she was supposed to meet Tom that morning."

It was nice to have confirmation of that. I continued. "The morning of the murder, she met with Tony and then fought with Tara. I don't know what exactly she did next, whether she went straight to the park or somewhere in between, but wherever she went, she ended up at the park, where I believe she was killed somewhere other than where I found her."

The chief's head popped up, and he stared at me. "Why do you think she was killed elsewhere? I haven't heard any rumors to that effect in town."

I grudgingly admired the way he avoided confirming that for me. "It stands to reason that if she died from a stab wound, there should have been a lot of blood, and I think I would have noticed that when I found her or when I saw the body once they moved the tree. I also think Louisa would have reacted to the smell of blood more."

"And how do you know she died from a stab wound?" he asked, not even trying to dissemble this time. He looked seriously disturbed that I had information that the police had been withholding.

"Believe it or not, my mother found out at the retirement home." I decided not to mention that I'd overheard him in his office.

"You have got to be kidding me!" His exasperation was evident on his face. "If I find out who leaked that, they will be in serious trouble!"

I hid a grin but decided I should at least protect the poor guy whose grandmother snooped. "The person who leaked it may not have done so intentionally. They can be a pretty sneaky lot at the retirement home, and they have a betting pool going on this."

The chief didn't look convinced, but I moved on.

"To me, the key is to find where Natalie put the thumb drive and to figure out what's on it, since I believe it led directly to her death. The problem is that if it were anywhere obvious, it would have already been found. I know Max has already been to The Grounds and Someone Else's Closet looking for it, and I assume he's searched their apartment, his office, and their cars."

"How do you know she didn't already turn it over to Tom or some other law enforcement officer?" Mike asked.

"Two reasons... One, if law enforcement had it, I think Max would have been arrested already. Two, I asked Tom about it, and he tried to cover, but he clearly hadn't known Natalie was going to give him a thumb drive." I turned to the chief. "I also assume that if you had found one on her body or near it, you would have turned the information over to Tom, and I'm sure after I told him, he must have asked you about it."

He shrugged and didn't comment.

I decided to push my luck a bit and asked, "Do you know where she was killed?"

He looked at me for a long time before answering, as if he was weighing each word carefully. Finally, he said, "Yes, we do. It was elsewhere in the park, but I'm not going to tell you where, so don't bother to ask. I can say, though, that there was no thumb drive found near there either."

I sighed. I really believed that if we could find the thumb drive, we could find the murderer. I needed to think it through some more.

"Was Natalie parked in one of the parking lots at the park?" I thought that might help me figure it out.

"No, her car was still behind her shop," the chief answered.

"Okay." I decided to wrap things up, as the day's events were catching up with me. Suddenly, I was exhausted. "I hope what I shared has helped you. I know you can't say anything, but I thought it was time that I told you everything I knew, just in case."

"I have to say I'm impressed with how much you've figured out. You gave me some information I didn't have. I'm not sure yet how it fits together, but I'm glad you trusted me enough to share." He looked at me, slightly exasperated, before continuing. "I know it will do no good to tell you to stop investigating, so I'm just going to ask you to be careful and let me know what you find out." He shook hands with all of us and thanked Lisa for dinner before heading out.

I headed to bed while Mike set the alarm. It had been a long, exhausting day, and I was discouraged and needed some rest. Hopefully, I'd have a better outlook in the morning.

Chapter Thirty

thought I would fall asleep quickly, as tired as I was, but I lay there a long time unable to get my brain to shut off. Then I had variations of the nightmare more than once, so when I woke up, I felt like I hadn't slept at all. As I was getting ready the next morning to go meet the security contractor, I realized that I hadn't heard from Tom at all yesterday. Not even a text. He'd been so attentive ever since we got shot at that I was a little surprised he hadn't at least sent me a text. I assumed he was busy with his case, but I had to confess, it made me feel like maybe he wasn't as interested in me as I thought he was. Louisa nudged my hand, and I shook off the negative feelings and headed down to let her out. Today, I would take my first step in taking back my life.

Mike had left a note on the table that he had to run to his office but would be back to pick me up by nine. That gave me plenty of time to feed myself and Louisa before he came back. I meant to ask Tom for any insights he had into what I should get for my security system, but now I thought that would have been presumptuous. I didn't really know him that well yet, and if he was no longer interested in me, asking him about something like the security system for my home might have made him uncomfortable. I was sure Mike could guide me through what I needed.

At nine on the dot, Mike pulled up out front, and we headed out to my house. There was an unfamiliar truck in the driveway when we arrived, and a tall man wearing navy coveralls and a ball cap came around the corner with a measuring tape. He introduced himself as Pete Walker of Walker Security. He and Mike already knew each other and chatted for a minute about how each was doing while I studied him. He had dark hair and chocolate brown eyes that exuded competence. He was in his mid-forties and had an ex-military vibe that matched Mike's. Mike soon verified that when he mentioned they had served together.

"So, Mrs. Douglas, I understand you are looking to put in some security out here," he said, getting down to business.

"You can call me Ellen." I smiled at him. "I think you should probably know there have been several attempts to break in at Mike and Lisa's since I started staying there. I've also been shot at. I'm not rich, but I want to feel safe in my own home. What do you suggest?"

He took me through a bunch of different options, with Mike weighing in on some he thought I really should have. "Besides the motion detectors, alarms on your doors and windows, and the cameras, you might want to consider putting up a gate across your driveway," Pete suggested.

"I'd have to fence the whole front yard then, wouldn't I?" I grimaced. "That sounds really expensive." I remembered how expensive it was when we fenced in the backyard for Louisa.

"That depends on what kind of fence you put up. Let me write up a quote, both with a fence and gate and without them," he said.

"How soon do you think you can give me an estimate and do the work?" I asked, anxious to get back into my home.

"I'll get an estimate to you today. The job would take one day without the gate. If we do the gate, we'll have to order the fencing and gate, so it would take about a week to come in and another two days to install. We can probably have you back in your home by Sunday if you're okay returning without the fence." He shook both our hands and went out to do some more measuring while we headed back to town.

"What do you think about the fence and the gate?" I asked Mike on the way back. "I mean, right now in the midst of this, I sort of want Fort Knox, but will it be overkill when they catch the killer, and things return to normal?"

"Maybe," he said thoughtfully. "But after all this, you may need Fort Knox to feel safe by yourself. I know you've been having nightmares, and I suspect you have some post-traumatic stress from all of this. I don't think that's going to go away immediately once the killer is caught. What you need to ask yourself is what will make you feel safe. If that's a fence and gate, then it's worth the peace of mind to have it. Just so you know, I told Pete I would help install everything, so he's going to give you a really good discount since he won't have to pay for a second person's labor on the job. And if it comes down to it and you really want the fence but feel like you can't afford it, Lisa and I will be glad to loan you the money. We want you to be safe and happy."

I felt myself tearing up, so touched by the support my friends were giving me. "I am so lucky to have such good friends," I said through a throat clogged with tears.

Pete was as good as his word and got me the estimate in the early afternoon. I was just going over it when the phone rang.

It was Tom!

"Hello," I said, trying to sound cool but feeling conflicted. I was happy he'd called but was trying not to read anything into it.

"Hi, Ellen." He sounded winded. "I'm sorry I didn't call yesterday. Are you okay? The chief sent me a copy of the police report about the intruder."

"I'm okay. Nothing really happened. He left pretty quickly."

"Things are really crazy here, but I hope to wrap it up by tomorrow at the latest. I'm so sorry I wasn't there yesterday for you. If I didn't believe what I was doing here would make you safer, I would turn around and head your way right now, but I really believe this is going to help clear all this up and make you safe again." He let out a long, drawn-out breath, and I felt my heart twinge. "Anything else going on there?"

"Mike and I met with a security contractor who is going to put in a security system at my house. I just got the estimate."

He asked several questions and told me he thought the gate and fence were a good idea, and he'd be happy to help build the fence if I wanted him to. I felt better after we hung up, but I needed to get my emotions under control where Tom was concerned. I couldn't keep doing this roller coaster every time he was out of touch for a bit. While I didn't know much about his job, I knew that it was an important one, and it needed to be his focus right now. Just as mine needed to be on finding a killer before anything else bad happened.

I called Pete and told him to go ahead with the main part of the security system, and we'd talk more about the fence after I'd given it some more thought. He promised to get with Mike and figure out what day for the installation worked for him. I hoped it would be tomorrow.

Chapter Thirty-One

had told Lisa I would take care of dinner tonight, so I headed into the kitchen to try to figure out what I wanted to make. I settled on making enchiladas and corn casserole and ordered the groceries I needed. While I waited for them to be delivered, I made myself some hot chocolate and sat down at the kitchen table to think.

I needed to make some decisions about what I wanted to do once the murder had been solved. I felt like I had just been reacting from one crisis to the next ever since I had found Natalie. Today's action to enhance security at my house was the first proactive thing I had done, and I realized I'd been sort of doing that in lots of areas of my life. I couldn't keep going on this way.

What did I want to do about becoming a partner in Someone Else's Closet? I had really enjoyed the two days I'd spent there. And I really liked Tara. We hadn't talked about the money yet, so that might be a problem, but I had good credit, so I could probably get a loan if I needed it to have enough to buy a partnership. I wasn't sure how tied down I would be.

Would I have to work every day? Even though my mother was pretty self-sufficient, she still needed me to take her places and handle her finances for her.

I really needed to sit down and have a serious conversation with Tara about some of my questions. I picked up my phone to send her a text message with a request to talk, but it rang before I could. It was Noelle.

"Hi, honey!" I said, happy to hear from her. "How was the interview?"

"It went really well, Mom. I'm pretty sure I'm going to get the internship." She sounded really excited.

"How long would you be in Louisville?" I was happy for her but sad I wouldn't be seeing her every few days like I could now.

"It's slated to last six months, with an option to extend to a year if things go well." She sounded like she was trying to tamp down her excitement, and I was afraid I hadn't hidden my ambivalence as well as I thought.

"I'm really happy for you, baby girl. And proud! This is quite an opportunity. Any chance you'll be able to get me tickets for the Kentucky Derby?" I joked. She knew that going to the Derby was on my bucket list.

She laughed. "I have no idea, but I'll make it happen if I can." She sounded lighter now.

"Are you having fun in Madison with your friends?"

"We found the best little coffee shop," she enthused, and it was my turn to laugh.

"Of course you did," I teased. "Did you make your own coffee?"

"Of course not," she said, feigning impatience. "Enough about me. How are you doing? Any other incidents?" She sounded concerned now.

"There was an intruder in the backyard, but Mike and the chief handled it quickly," I said, trying to sound nonchalant so she wouldn't worry more than she already was. "I called a security company, and they are going to install some cameras and other things at the house. I'm ready to go home."

"Don't be in too much of a rush, Mom!" She still sounded worried. "Why don't you at least wait until they arrest someone before you go home?"

"I hate to be a burden to Lisa and Mike any longer than necessary, although they haven't said anything at all. I'm lucky to have such good friends."

"They are lucky to have you, too, Mom," she said loyally. The line became muffled for a minute, and I heard her talking with someone else, but I couldn't hear what she was saying. "Sorry, Mom. I have to go. Call me if you need me. Otherwise, I have to work on Sunday, so I'll stop and see you after I get done."

"Have a good time! I'll see you then! Love you!" After I hung up, I felt lighter. Talking to my daughter often had that effect.

The groceries came soon after, and as I prepared the food, I contemplated the other major decision I needed to make. Did I want to pursue a relationship with Tom? I really enjoyed spending time with him, but a lot of our interactions were surrounding the current murder investigation. When that was no longer going on, was there enough to base a relationship on?

I had just put the enchiladas in to bake when Lisa came in from work. She came and sat down at the table with me. "Smells good. I love your enchiladas!"

I smiled. "I know. That's why I made them. I can't tell you how much I appreciate all you and Mike have done for me this week!"

"You are my best friend," she said. "In fact, you are essentially family. I would do anything to make sure you were safe."

I teared up a bit and reached over to squeeze her hand.

"So, Mike told me what the security guy said. Did you decide to go for it?"

"Yes. I already sent him a deposit so he could start ordering supplies."

She looked at me, and because she knew me almost better than I knew myself, she quickly figured out I had something on my mind. "Do you want to talk about it?"

I started to deflect but then decided to just ask what I wanted to know. "How did you know it was time to start dating again after your divorce?"

She thought for a minute before replying. "It wasn't just a decision to date. It was a decision to date Mike specifically. I know you know the basics of our story, but really, we were friends first."

"So how did you know it was time to become more than friends?" I asked. Strangely, we had never talked about this before. She hadn't introduced me to Mike until they had been dating for months. I was shocked when she told me they were getting married.

"It wasn't a decision I made easily. I had been so hurt by the end of my marriage that it was really difficult to trust someone again. But Mike was super patient with me. And I finally acknowledged that I missed being part of a couple. I missed the companionship. I missed having someone to make decisions with." I nodded, because I missed those things too.

"What sealed it for me was when Molly had her accident, and we weren't sure if she was going to make it." Molly was her daughter, and she'd been in a terrible car accident about three years ago. She'd suffered a traumatic brain injury and had been in a coma for about a week. "Mike was a rock for me through that whole thing. You were too, but you're my best friend; you had to be. But if it had been my ex, he would have left me to take care of everything alone. Mike showed up and did anything I needed."

"I remember." I squeezed her hand again. "So do you think Tom is someone I should let into my life?"

"I like him," she said, "and I think you are lonelier than you like to admit. I don't know if he is Mr. Right or just someone for right now, but I think it wouldn't hurt to give him a chance."

I nodded. She had given me a lot to think about.

Over dinner, the three of us talked over the prospect of my becoming a partner in Someone Else's Closet. As a small business owner, Mike had some really good insights into things I should ask. We lingered at the table just talking for a long time.

Mike excused himself to take a call and came back smiling. "Ellen, that was Pete. He was able to pick up everything he needed for the initial hardware at your house. He and I were both free, so we're going to do the install tomorrow."

I sighed with relief. "That is amazing! Thank you so much!"

"I thought you might want to take that opportunity to be home for a day. Since we'll be there all day, it should be safe." He grinned at the bright smile that had come over my face.

"I would love that. I'm sure at the very least my house needs to be cleaned." I felt something inside me loosen at the thought of being back in my own space, even if it was only for a few hours.

"Why don't I plan on bringing everyone lunch?" Lisa suggested. "That will save Mike and Pete time, and no one will have to leave, which will be safer."

We all agreed that it was a great idea, and I decided that if we were going to be leaving early, I should head up to bed. I hugged them both goodnight and went up to my room to get ready for bed. After I crawled into bed, I grabbed my notebook off the nightstand and jotted down some notes on what I wanted to ask Tara when we met next week. I was afraid I would forget some of the things Mike had suggested when we talked earlier. I was just about asleep when my phone dinged. It was a text from Tom.

Thinking of you. I hope I'll be back on Sunday around noon.

I had decided if I was going to give him a fair shot, I should be honest about how I was feeling, so I replied.

I'm really looking forward to seeing you! Be safe!

Sunday was just the day after tomorrow. I would try not to be too impatient.

—————————— ❧ ——————————

Chapter Thirty-Two

Saturday morning dawned sunny, cool, and windy with a little bite of fall in the air. Lisa, bless her heart, had gotten up early and made breakfast sandwiches wrapped in foil so we could head out right away. Pete was meeting us out there at seven, so Mike and I grabbed the bag of sandwiches, a thermos of coffee, and Louisa and headed out the door. I rode with Mike instead of taking my own car, since we were worried someone was still watching me. Louisa easily jumped up into Mike's truck, and I was happy to see she was healing well enough to do so without a whimper.

When we arrived, Pete was already there, so I took my breakfast and Louisa and headed into the house. It had that stale smell houses got that had sat empty for a while. And it was chilly, so I decided to light a fire to both warm and cheer things up. I used some scented pinecones as fire starters, and soon the aroma of cinnamon and cedar began to permeate the house. I made some hot chocolate and ate my sausage and egg biscuit in a chair close to the fire. It felt like it had been an eternity since I had last been there, not just a few days.

So much had happened in that time, and I suspected I was a different person than the one who had drunk tea and had an awkward conversation here with Tom just a few days ago.

Could it really have only been a few days? That seemed impossible in so many ways. I had always loved sitting by a fire, whether it was in a fire pit outside or a fireplace inside. I found it soothing, so I sat and savored the peace for a while with Louisa curled up nearby on the hearthrug. I found myself relaxing into my safe place. I had been living with a constant low level of anxiety humming through me for a week without realizing it until I noticed it was gone. I'd needed this!

Finally, I decided I'd better be productive, since I was hoping to move back in tonight if they finished the installation today. It would be heaven to sleep in my own bed. I let Louisa out in the backyard after making sure Mike and Pete weren't working out there. I figured I should let her run while she could, since I didn't want her to bother them when they moved to the back.

Then I pulled out my cleaning supplies and started in the family room. Dog hair had a way of accumulating, and Louisa often tracked in leaves from the yard. I normally had the robot vacuum cleaner run every few days, but today I decided it needed a deeper cleaning. And I hoped the activity would keep my brain from bringing back the worry. I dusted and swept the family room and then moved to the kitchen area.

I opened the fridge to get a drink and discovered my strawberries were fuzzy, so I ended up going through everything and getting rid of perishables that hadn't survived my absence. By the time I finished cleaning the kitchen and living room, it was nearly lunchtime, so I pulled out some paper plates and set the table in preparation for Lisa's arrival with lunch.

At noon on the dot, I heard Louisa barking and went to the front door to see Lisa walking up with two huge bags of food. Mike and Pete came in and washed up at the kitchen sink, and we all sat down to the feast Lisa had brought.

"This is enough food for an army," I teased her. "Just how many people did you think you were feeding?"

"I know how men are when they're doing a physical job," she stated, unfazed by my teasing. "You'll see. They're going to eat most of this, and you can have the leftovers for another meal."

"So how are things going?" I asked Mike.

"Really well. We've gotten the cameras and motion detectors mostly installed out front."

Pete added, "Another thirty minutes, and we should be ready to move to the back. You might want to bring your dog in then."

"I'll bring her in right after lunch," I assured him. "I just didn't want her bothering you while you ate. She's very good at begging, even though she's never successful in getting me to give her anything."

We all laughed.

Lisa stayed until lunch was cleaned up and then headed home to do her own house cleaning. I let Louisa in, and she headed straight back to the hearth rug. I had been periodically adding wood to the fire, so it was nice and toasty there. She would probably nap there all afternoon. I was tempted to join her, but I wanted to finish cleaning first.

I decided to tackle my room next, and then I would just have the bathrooms left to do. I pulled off my sheets and threw them in to wash while I put on clean ones. As I was vacuuming, I noticed a lot of smudges on my windows and thought, *Next nice day, I'm going to need to wash those.* It was too cold today, and I was getting tired. Too many nights with too little sleep were catching up to me, I guessed, since house-cleaning didn't normally wipe me out like this. I had to force myself not to crawl into my freshly made bed and forget about the bathrooms.

When I walked into my ensuite, I felt the blood drain from my face, and the air froze in my lungs. Someone had used lipstick to write, *You should have listened!* on the mirror above my sink. I felt the scream building in my throat, but managed to control it and pulled out my cell phone instead. I took a picture and texted it to both the chief and Mike with the caption, *Someone has been in my house.* And then I just stood there numbly staring at it until Mike came running in.

"Ellen, are you all right?" He looked at me like I was a glass that might shatter if he touched me.

"Why does this keep happening?" I asked him, wide-eyed. "And how did they get in?"

"The chief is on his way. He'll figure it out. For right now, why don't you come in by the fire?" he suggested, taking my arm and leading me out of the room.

I realized I was shivering uncontrollably, and he piled more logs on the fire and wrapped a blanket around me while we waited for Chief Andrews.

As if sensing my distress, Louisa came and put her head on my lap, whining quietly. I stroked her fur and thought about how, all the time I had been feeling safe here in my home, someone had already violated my sanctuary. I wondered if I would ever feel safe anywhere again.

Chapter Thirty-Three

hief Andrews arrived with an army of police, including sheriff's deputies and crime scene techs, in addition to his own officers. My house was outside the city limits, but there was a mutual support agreement for our part of the county. Since all the related crimes had occurred in Cascade, the sheriff's office was allowing the chief to take the lead in this investigation as well.

I was very grateful, as I wasn't sure I could handle dealing with someone else at this point.

When he came in, Chief Andrews crouched down next to me and patted me on the arm. "How are you holding up?"

I grimaced. "Not well. I have always felt safe here, and now I know that was an illusion." I knew I sounded bitter, but I felt entitled to be bitter about this invasion of my home.

"You will feel safe here again once they get all the security in place. Mike told me you were planning to move back here tonight if they finished the security system. I'm sorry, but your house is now a crime scene, so I'm afraid they can't continue the installation until we have processed the scene. That is going to take several hours, so I'm going to need you to go back to the Partridges' after I take your statement. Mike promised to drive you back as soon as we're done."

My shoulders slumped. "To be honest, I'm not sure I would have been okay out here alone tonight after this anyway."

He smiled gently. "I think most people would feel that way. Ellen, I need you to tell me in detail what you did when you got here today."

I thought longingly for a minute of sitting here by the fire earlier with my hot chocolate. "I came in and built a fire because it was chilly in here. Then I made a drink in the kitchen and had breakfast. After I sat there for a while, I decided to clean, and I worked on this end of the house until Lisa brought lunch. Then we all ate, and I started working on my bedroom."

"And that's when you found the mirror?" he asked.

I nodded.

"Did you touch anything in the bathroom?"

"No." I shook my head. "I saw it as soon as I stepped through the doorway and never went farther."

"While you were cleaning, did you notice anything unusual?" His eyes were penetrating. "Anything at all."

"I noticed the window in my room had a lot of fingerprints. I was thinking it needed to be washed. Other than that, I can't think of anything." I shrugged.

"Were the doors locked?"

"I know the back sliding door was, and the garage door was closed when we got here, but I never looked at the front door." I frowned in thought.

"What about the windows?" he asked.

"I never checked them today. I know I locked them before I left with Lisa, because I was a little freaked out that someone might be watching me."

He looked up sharply from where he had been taking notes. "You thought someone might have been watching you that long ago?"

I nodded. "It was more a feeling than anything concrete, and I thought at the time I was probably freaked out about the message on my car."

"What made you think someone might be watching you?" He was frowning.

"Tom had brought me home that day, and when he left, I thought I caught a glimpse of someone over in the trees. It was more the impression of something there than didn't belong than seeing an actual person."

"Can you show me where approximately they were?" He helped me up and led me out the garage door to the driveway.

I pointed to where I had seen something in the trees. "Right over there behind those large trees at the edge of the yard."

He called over a couple of his officers and pointed, but I didn't hear what he said to them, because Mike walked up and asked me, "How are you doing?"

I gave him a shaky smile. "Better than ten minutes ago, but not as good as two hours ago."

He laughed.

Chief Andrews turned back to us. "I think that's all I need for right now, Ellen, so if you want to collect Louisa and head back to Mike and Lisa's, I'll come by when we finish here and give you an update."

I asked tentatively, "Is there any way I could grab a few more clothes from my room? I didn't really expect to be gone for as long as I have been." I didn't want to cause a problem with the crime scene, but I would love some other outfits to wear.

"Since you've already cleaned in there, I don't guess that should be too much of a problem. I'll have Officer Lyndsey take you in, and once you've packed, she'll need to take your fingerprints for elimination purposes." He gestured to a young woman standing a few feet away.

"My fingerprints are on file with the federal government since I was fingerprinted for my job. Would you have access to those?" I'd always been curious about that.

"We do, through the FBI's Next Generation Identification system." The chief addressed Officer Lyndsey. "You won't need to get her fingerprints, but can you still escort her in to get some clothes and her dog?" He turned back and said, "I'll be by to see you as soon as we're done, and we'll make sure everything is locked up tight when we leave."

I thanked him, went inside, and quickly packed for a few more days. When I came back out, Mike had already loaded Louisa into the car, and he put my bag in the back with her before climbing into the truck and heading us toward Cascade.

On the way back to town, I texted Noelle to let her know that they weren't going to finish the install today, so I would be at the Partridges' again tonight. I didn't tell her about the break-in or the warning. I figured tomorrow was soon enough to tell her about them, and I didn't want to ruin the last day of her getaway with her friends. She sent me back a thumbs-up emoji, and I was glad she was distracted enough not to ask me any details, because I didn't want to lie to her.

Then, before I could talk myself out of it, I sent a text to Tom.

Can you talk?

He didn't respond immediately.

Lisa met us at the door and pulled me in for a hug.

I felt the weight of the day descend, and I burst into tears. I cried on her shoulder for a few moments before I pulled back and dried my eyes with my hand. I smiled tremulously at her. "Thanks. I needed that."

"That's what friends are for," she said, squeezing my hand. "Now, what can I do to help? Are you hungry? Do you want to watch a movie? What would make you feel better?"

"To be honest, my head is killing me, and I think I'd just like to lie down for a while. Is that okay?" I didn't want her to feel like I was rejecting her offer of companionship, but I really needed to be alone for a bit.

"Of course it's okay," she reassured me. "You go lie down, and I'll come check on you when dinner is ready. I put some chicken in the slow cooker, but it will be a couple of hours before it's ready. I planned for a late dinner because I expected the install to take a while. Do you need some meds?"

"I have something upstairs I can take, but I think I may just try to sleep off the headache." I gave her a tired smile and headed upstairs to my room.

I kicked off my shoes and slid under the covers. Just as I was about asleep, my phone rang. It was Tom!

"Ellen?" His voice sounded so good that I almost burst into tears for the second time in ten minutes. "Sorry, I couldn't call right away. I was in a meeting. I called as soon as it ended."

"That's okay. I hope I'm not interrupting," I said, thinking I shouldn't have asked him to call, but just hearing his voice made me feel so much better.

"Everything okay?" he asked.

"Not really," I admitted. "When we were at my house today, we discovered someone had broken in and left another message," I told him about finding the mirror.

"Oh, Ellen, I'm so sorry." Sympathy oozed from his voice. "I wish I were there. I'm close to finishing what I'm doing here. I still think I'll be back by about noon tomorrow."

"I know you're busy, so I'll let you go, but I didn't want you to hear about this from someone else."

"I'm really glad you called, Ellen," he said warmly. "You can call me anytime you need me."

We hung up, and I lay there in bed, warmth filling me from the inside out. I knew our relationship was in its beginning stages, but hearing his voice and knowing he cared about me made me feel better. I fell asleep thinking about how nice it would be when he got back.

Chapter Thirty-Four

isa gently shook me awake. "The chief just arrived and wants to talk to you."

I had been deeply asleep and felt groggy. My head was still killing me, too. "Tell him I'll be right down," I told her and then headed for the bathroom to brush my hair and find some ibuprofen.

When I got downstairs, Lisa had dinner ready. She insisted that the chief eat with us, so we settled around the kitchen table. By unspoken agreement, we just chit-chatted during dinner. Lisa had made chicken and pasta in a creamy cheese sauce. She served it with garlic bread and a salad. The chief ate heartily, and I suspected he didn't get a home-cooked meal very often. Lisa, Mike, and I regularly had dinner either at my house or here. I'd have to invite him to join us sometimes when this was all over.

Once dinner was over, the chief, Mike, and I retired to the living room to talk while Lisa cleaned up dinner.

I offered to help her, but she waved me away. "Don't worry about it. There isn't much cleanup to do. I'll put the leftovers away, and everything else can go in the dishwasher."

I agreed, although I was reluctant to hear what the chief had to tell me. I felt like I was waiting for the other shoe to drop.

I settled onto the couch with Louisa lying beside me, her head on my lap. Mike and the chief each took a chair facing me, so we formed a sort of triangle.

I looked at the chief and smiled grimly. "Okay, out with it. I could tell the minute I saw you that you had news I was not going to like."

He smiled sheepishly. "I'm afraid you're right. Let's start with the warning in the house. It appears they got in by jimmying open your bedroom window. It didn't break the lock, but you'll probably want to engage the features on your windows that don't allow them to open all the way."

It was my turn to look sheepish. "I don't have it on because a couple of times I've gotten locked out and had to climb in through a window."

Mike gave me a stern look. "You won't be doing that again. When the new system is fully installed, you won't need to anyway. You can use the smart locks from your phone or the garage keypad, even if the power is out." He turned to the chief. "I'll make sure the windows all have the safety feature engaged when we put the alarms on them."

The chief continued. "We lifted several fingerprints off the pane, and we're running them through the FBI's system to see if they match any known criminals, but that often takes a few days. The message appears to have been written using lipstick. Do you recognize this?" He held out a plastic evidence bag with a small pink tube in it.

I looked at it and then at the color name on the bottom. "I'm pretty sure this is mine. It's my brand and a color I know I've used. My tube would have been in the drawer of the vanity."

He nodded. "We thought it was probably yours, which seems to indicate that the intent for breaking in was not necessarily to leave a warning. If it had been, they would likely have brought their own writing instrument."

"Why do you think they broke in?" Mike asked, leaning forward.

"We don't know for sure, because we aren't sure when the break-in happened. It could have been any time since Ellen moved over here." He turned back to me. "You haven't been home at all, have you?"

I shook my head. "No, I haven't been back since Lisa picked me up there several days ago."

"So, they might have broken in to see if they could figure out where Ellen had gone and then used the opportunity to give her another warning," the chief speculated.

"But that wouldn't make sense," I interjected. "They wouldn't have known at that point that I was still asking questions."

He nodded in acknowledgement. "The other possibility is they broke in days later, looking either for Ellen or for something Ellen had at her home. Can you think of anything they might have been looking for, Ellen?"

I thought for a moment. "There are only two things associated with the case that I know someone has been looking for. One is the missing flash drive Max has been looking all over town for, and the other is a piece of paper with what we think is Max's key for his cryptocurrency wallet. The flash drive is still missing, but the paper has been returned to Max."

"So maybe someone went looking for the drive in your house," Mike said thoughtfully.

"Did you notice anything out of place when you were cleaning, Ellen?" the chief asked.

"Not that I can think of." I shook my head. "If anything, it seemed neater than normal because I hadn't been there to do laundry and get the mail."

"That may mean," the chief said, looking concerned, "that we are dealing with a professional. Someone who can search without leaving a trace is likely very dangerous."

I quaked at the thought.

"Unfortunately, we found something else that has me concerned." He looked at me. "Do you remember what you said about thinking you saw someone when Tom left that day?"

I nodded. "Of course. Did you find something?" I wasn't sure I wanted to hear the answer.

"The deputies did a thorough sweep of the entire property, and they found where someone had clearly been watching your house for a long time. There were multiple cigarette butts, empty pop cans, and there were holes in the ground that looked like they might fit a camping stool or some other kind of chair."

"So I wasn't being paranoid," I whispered, creeped out that someone had been watching me. "Any idea how long they had been there?"

"No." He frowned. "And we aren't sure the watcher is who broke into the house. There were some distinct shoe prints in the woods and under your window in the flower bed, and they didn't match."

Mike's eyes got big. "So two people are stalking her?"

"Maybe?" the chief said uncertainly. "We really don't know. Which leads me to ask… How far did you get on the install today, Mike? Any chance you have anything active yet?"

"Actually, yes. We were able to complete the front yard cameras and motion detectors before we had to stop."

I looked at him in surprise. "I didn't realize you got that far."

"I wasn't planning to activate it until we did the rest of the install, but I can turn it on remotely right now if you'd like me to." Mike pulled out his laptop.

"I would like a heads-up if someone comes back out there, so if you don't mind, Ellen, I think he should turn it on." He and Mike both looked at me.

"I agree," I said, feeling more decisive. "Let's see if anyone is still lurking. I think I'll feel better knowing one way or the other."

Mike typed on his computer for a couple of minutes and then looked up. "All set. I'll get an alert if any motion is detected out there tonight."

"You'll let me know if you get one, right?" the chief asked.

"Of course," Mike agreed.

"Ellen, I know this hasn't been the day you were expecting, but I honestly think this may help us figure out who is behind all of this." The chief stood. "I'm going to let you get some rest, but we'll touch base tomorrow afternoon."

"Thank you for everything!" I started to stand, but he waved me down.

Mike walked him out, and I assumed they must have had a conversation, because he didn't come back for a while. By the time he came back inside, Lisa had joined me on the couch, and we decided to watch a game show. I found myself dozing off about halfway through, so I thought I'd turn in early.

I thanked them both again and started for the stairs, but Mike followed me into the hall. "The chief says we can continue work on the security system tomorrow. It will only take us a few hours to finish up, but I think you should still consider staying here with us until these people are caught."

I gave him a tired smile. "Thanks, Mike. I'll plan to stay here for at least a couple more days if you're sure you're okay with it."

"You can stay with us as long as you want," he assured me. "We love having you here. I just wish the circumstances were different."

We said good night, and I dragged myself up the stairs. I really needed some rest.

Chapter Thirty-Five

woke with a start from a vivid dream where someone was chasing me through the forest. It was the familiar trail I always took, but it was dark, and I kept stumbling over roots I couldn't see. Suddenly, up ahead was the fork where I'd found Natalie, but this time, instead of finding her body, I was grabbed from behind by whoever was following me, and they plunged a huge knife into my chest. I guess it was the pain that woke me up. And I rubbed my chest because it still felt like it was hurting where the person in my dream had stabbed me.

Then I started to cough, and I realized the pain in my chest might be something more than the residual effects of a bad dream. I couldn't be sick! I didn't have time for this, and if I was sick, I wanted to be in my own bed in my own home. I dragged myself to the bathroom and searched for some cold medicine in my toiletries bag. There was only one dose left in the package, so I was going to have to get some more tomorrow if this lingered. I took the medicine and headed back to bed, but lying flat, I couldn't breathe, so I ended up propped up on all the pillows. Half sitting, I fell into a fitful sleep. I had several more dreams of being spied on or chased, and I didn't feel rested at all when my alarm went off the next morning.

I normally didn't like to ask for help, but I felt so bad that I sent a text to Noelle, asking if she could bring me some hot tea and cold meds when she got a chance. She promised to bring them over on her first break and told me to stay in bed and rest. She had just replied when I heard a tap at the door.

"Come in," I croaked, and Lisa stuck her head in, looking concerned.

"That cough sounds terrible." She came over and felt my head. "And I'm pretty sure you have a fever. Do you want me to take you to an immediate care clinic or your doctor?"

I shook my head. "It's probably just my sinuses or a cold. Noelle is bringing me tea and meds."

"I could have done that for you," she said with a tsk.

"You guys have already done so much." I started coughing again.

She frowned. "We're friends. We take care of each other. I'm going to make you some toast and bring up some water and cough drops before I go to work. You just rest!"

She left with Louisa before I could reply, and I sank back into the pillows. I must have fallen back asleep, because when I was next aware, there was a glass of water, some toast, and a bunch of cough drops on the nightstand, and Louisa was curled up next to me on the bed, snoozing.

I realized that my phone was ringing and tried to answer, but my voice came out as a whisper. "Hello?"

"Ellen?" My mother's voice boomed over the phone, and I had to pull it away from my ear. "You sound terrible. What's wrong with you?"

"I think I have a cold," I said, managing to eke out a little more volume than when I originally answered.

"You need some good old-fashioned chicken soup," she prescribed. "Too bad I don't have what I need in my kitchen to whip you up some of mine. Well, if you're sick, you probably don't want to hear the other news I was calling about."

"No, it's okay," I rasped. "I can listen better than I can talk."

"Well, if you're sure… I thought you'd want to know that Martha's daughter saw Natalie the morning she died. We were talking about the murder after bingo, and her daughter was here visiting. She said Natalie was entering the park by the playground when she saw her, and she thought Natalie was acting strangely."

"How so?" I asked, intrigued despite how bad I felt.

"She said Natalie kept looking over her shoulder and then all around, like she was either looking for someone or thought someone was following her. Then, a few minutes later, when she was driving by the falls, she saw Natalie bent down to tie her shoe over on the rocks at the side of the falls. Martha's daughter said Natalie was looking around so much, it took her a long time to tie her shoe."

"She didn't say what time this was, did she?"

"She didn't remember exactly but said it was midmorning sometime."

I thought about that. The timing seemed right. I felt like this should tell me something, but my brain was so mushy from the fever and the cold that I couldn't grasp it.

"Oh, that's the activities director knocking on my door. Feel better soon! And if you want me to come over and make you some chicken soup, let me know." She hung up before I could even say goodbye.

What surprised me most about that call was that my mother apparently hadn't heard about the break-in at my house. I would have to tell her eventually, but I wasn't sure I had the energy today.

A few minutes later, I heard a tap at my door, and Noelle came in with tea and a pharmacy bag. "Oh, Mom, you look like you feel terrible."

I managed a weak smile as I reached to take the cup from her. "I do feel pretty rotten. How did you get in? I didn't hear you knock."

"I texted Lisa, and she opened the garage door remotely for me so I didn't have to wake you if you were asleep."

"Ah, that was smart," I said. "Thank you, sweetheart! What kind of tea did you bring me?"

"Ginger with honey and lemon. I figured that would soothe your throat from the coughing." She held out the pharmacy bag. "And in here, I have a decongestant, cough medicine, and cough drops, although I see you already have some of those."

"Thank you, honey." I took the bag and looked inside. "There's some cash in my purse downstairs."

She waved that away and sat down in a chair near the bed. "Are you sure you shouldn't go to the doctor?"

"I think it's just a cold, but if I'm feeling worse, I'll go to the doctor tomorrow," I promised. Suddenly, I knew what was significant about the spot where Natalie was tying her shoe. "Do you remember when your dad and I used to take you geocaching?"

"Ugh! Yes. All those hikes through the weeds or on trails looking for a needle in a haystack." She smiled. "Although I did like it when we placed one of our own, and would check on it to see what people had left there. Remember that silver whistle I got one time and a really cool pin another time that I put on my backpack?"

I grinned at the nostalgia in her voice. I was glad she had liked at least part of our adventures. "Do you ever hear any-one talking about geocaching anymore? I haven't thought about it in a very long time."

"Now that you mention it, I did hear someone talking about it at The Grounds one day recently. They had found one in the park and were trying to describe to the person they were with how hard it was to find. I remember commenting on it to Natalie and Tara, who were at the counter, because it was one we had placed when I was a kid. I was surprised it was still there. They were fascinated because neither of them had ever gone geocaching."

"Do you mean the one by the falls?" I asked, suddenly feeling more awake.

"Yes, that one was hardly ever found. I think we hid it too well. What made you think of geocaching?" she asked curiously. "We haven't talked about that in years!"

"I don't know, really. Something your grandmother said on the phone made me think of it." I didn't want to give her the context, but I also didn't want to lie to my daughter.

"Good times. All right, do you need anything else before I go? I have to get back." She picked up her purse and stood.

I started to let her go but decided I'd better tell her about the warning before someone else did. "Sweetheart, when we were at the house yesterday for the security install, we dis-covered someone had broken in while I was staying here."

She sat back down. "Was anything taken?"

"Not that I could tell. They left me another warning on the mirror in my bathroom." I started coughing again and couldn't keep talking.

"You'd better rest," she said, standing up again. "You can tell me the rest later."

"Thanks for bringing all this for me," I croaked out be-tween coughs.

She left, and I pulled out the meds, hurried to the bath-room, and started the shower. If I was right, I knew where the flash drive was, and I needed to get to it before someone else did.

⚜

Chapter Thirty-Six

fter a steamy shower, more meds, and eating the toast, I felt a little better. I thought the shower had brought my fever down enough that I should be okay making a short trip to the park. I decided to walk, since I wasn't sure I should drive, as foggy as I felt. Just as I was walking out the door, my phone rang again. It was Tom.

"Hello," I said, trying to make my voice as normal as possible.

"Hi! I wanted to let you know that I'm on my way back. I should be in town in about twenty minutes. Would you like to have lunch?" He sounded eager to see me.

"Actually, could you meet me at the falls in the park?" I started coughing, but I hoped he'd heard me. I popped in a cough drop.

"It sounds like you should be in bed, not going to the park." The concern in his voice touched me.

"I don't think this can wait," I said. "I think I know where the flash drive is, and if I'm right, it could be found by some stranger and taken away at any time, and we'll never know what's on it."

"I really think you should wait for me to get there, and you can tell me where it is," he said, but in my feverish brain, all I could think of was finding it as fast as I could.

"You'd never find it without my help," I said as I turned into the park entrance. "I helped hide something in that spot in the first place, and I still have trouble finding it. Besides, I'm almost to the falls. I promise that once I find it, I'll wait on one of the benches until you get there."

"Ellen, someone has been actively trying to scare you, at the least, and possibly hurt you," he protested.

"There will be tons of people in the park, and I'll just be by the falls. He's only ever approached me when I've been alone, and I won't be alone in that part of the park." I hung up before he could protest any more. My feverish brain was hyper-focused on getting to that geocache, and I couldn't think about anything else.

I made my way through the playground and across the picnic area to the falls. It was a beautiful day, and the playground was full of parents with their preschoolers. Several families were also feeding the ducks, and I smiled at the ones I knew but didn't stop to talk. I could feel myself dragging from the walk, and my breath was coming in gasps, but I knew I could rest once I got to the falls.

On either side of the bridge over the falls, some rocks provided a floodplain for the creek when the water got too high for its banks. A little farther off to one side was a series of steps that were used when this part of the creek was a swimming area in the mid-twentieth century. I moved across the rocks to where the steps started. There was an overhang there that made a small cavity. I reached in and pulled out a small waterproof plastic box that was about three inches by five inches. Just as I was about to open it, I heard something, so I shoved it back in and casually slid around as if I'd come here to sit on the steps and not access the box.

To my right, I saw a muscular man dressed all in black. He was balding and had tattoos peaking up from his shirt collar. He was staring at me intently, and I started to get really nervous. I jumped up and darted to the bridge. If I could get to the other side, surely I could lose him in the woods.

My phone rang just as I reached the opposite side of the bridge. It was Tom again.

"Where are you? I just got to the park, and I don't see your car."

I glanced back and saw that the man in black was gaining on me.

I hurried on and whispered into the phone, "I think someone is following me. I just crossed the bridge over the falls, and I'm heading into the woods on the other side. I'm going to try to lose him in the woods."

"Stay on the line with me," he said urgently. "I'm going to click over and call the police. Don't hang up! I'll be right back."

I put my phone in my pocket so I could scramble up the hill. On the other side of the hill, the trail split. If I could get down one of the paths fast enough, he'd have to spend some time looking for me. Unfortunately, when I reached the top, I was so out of breath that I had a hard time hurrying. I could feel a coughing fit coming on and reached into my pocket for another cough drop, hoping to stave it off. It would be easy to find me if I were coughing up a lung.

My head was swimming, and I could feel myself weakening. If I could just keep moving until Tom found me, I would be okay. Suddenly, a man stepped out of the shadows onto the trail directly in front of me. I stopped in my tracks and then realized it was Max!

"Do you have it?" he asked urgently.

I stared at him uncomprehendingly.

"The flash drive?" He was very agitated, and I instinctively started to back away from him, forgetting about the man who was following me for a minute. Max reached out and grabbed my arm. "I'm trying to help you!" His gaze darted behind me, as if he were looking for the other man. "If you give me the flash drive, they'll leave you alone."

"I don't have it," I whispered, as frightened as I'd ever been in my life.

"But you know where it is. I know you do!" He pulled me to the side of the trail into some trees and shook me. "You have to tell me, or they'll kill us both." He was frantic now, and I wondered if I would be better off taking my chances with the man in black. I decided to try to placate him, since his grip on my arm was so tight that I didn't think I could get away from him.

"I think I know where it is," I admitted. "But before I could confirm it, a bald man dressed all in black interrupted me, so I'm not sure."

He cursed. "We have to get that drive, or we're both dead. Where is it?"

"Near the falls on the other side of the creek." I decided that was as specific as I should be at this point if I wanted him to keep me alive. I knew Tom was listening to our conversation, so I hoped that would help him locate us. "We can't go back that way," I said, looking back in the direction from which I'd come, "because the man followed me into the woods."

"We'll have to go to the other bridge and go around," he began, dragging me along the trail in the direction of the other bridge and parking area where I normally began my walks. I knew this part of the path well and tried to figure out if there was anywhere I might have a chance of getting away from him. We were rapidly approaching the spot where I'd found Natalie's body.

"Why did you kill her?" I asked, trying to sound conversational rather than accusing.

He jerked my arm, stopped on the trail, and stared at me. The devastation I saw on his face surprised me. I had decided he was a cold-blooded killer, but maybe he had really cared for Natalie.

"I didn't mean to kill her." He began dragging me forward along the trail again. "I just needed the drive back. If she had given it to me, I would have forgiven her and taken her back. Why did she have to take it?" He looked at me as if I should be able to answer that.

"But she had hidden it before you caught up with her in the woods?" I prompted.

"She wouldn't tell me where it was. I was just so angry that I pulled out my letter opener and held it to her throat. I wouldn't have hurt her; it was just so she would talk to me.

But then she started fighting me, and somehow it stabbed her. I tried to stop the bleeding, but there was too much." He looked haunted, but I told myself that this was a murderer and I needed to keep my guard up.

"So why did you move her body?" I was really curious about this point, as I had no idea why.

"I wanted her found far away from where I'd parked my car, and I wasn't sure if I had left anything the cops could find where she died, so I carried her down the trail and then broke off a large branch. I was hoping that maybe if it appeared to be an accident, they wouldn't look too much harder." By this point, we had reached the place where I had found Natalie's body. I could see where the flowers had been, but I guessed the police had taken the teddy bear and the note.

"Did you leave the memorial here?" I asked.

He stopped moving for a moment and nodded. "I really did love her, you know. If she had just stayed out of my business, we could have been married and lived happily ever after."

He started hurrying me along again, but my strength was flagging as the initial adrenaline rush began to subside. He was pretty much dragging me down the trail now, and I felt myself falling. He caught me before I hit the ground, but he shook me until my teeth rattled. "What is wrong with you? We have to hurry. Get up." His eyes were crazed, and he was both furious and terrified. He kept looking behind me for the man in black.

"I'm sorry!" I gasped and started coughing. "I've been really sick, and I need to stop and rest for a moment. Please!" I begged, both because I was exhausted and to give Tom time to find us.

He let me sit for a minute to catch my breath, and I asked him, "What's on that drive, anyway? And why did you think I had it?"

"It's a ledger showing the ownership of all the crypto wallets where I receive transactions and who owns the wallets I send them to." he snapped.

"So why does the man in black want it so bad?" I asked, not quite sure I understood.

"He's from the cartel. They think I've been skimming money off the top, and the ledger would allow them to figure it out. Not to mention what would happen to all of us if the Feds got ahold of it!" He was practically foaming at the mouth by the time he finished explaining.

He took a breath, and I could see him physically trying to calm down. When he spoke next, he sounded more in control. "Since you found the paper at Someone Else's Closet, I figured there was a good chance you knew where the drive was, too."

"Honestly, I just figured that out this morning," I said. I was trying to keep my voice steady, but I could hear a slight wobble.

His head jerked back at the snap of a branch that seemed really close. Without a word, he grabbed my arm, hauled me to my feet, and hissed at me to be quiet. We started moving down the trail again quietly, going as fast as I could manage. He kept glancing behind, but the man in black never came into view. I was getting winded again, and I wasn't sure how much longer I could keep up this pace.

We were rapidly approaching the other bridge and came to a clearing where two trails met. Several things happened all at once. Chief Andrews stepped out in front of us on the trail, and the man who had been following us came up behind us.

Max pulled me in front of him and held me as a shield while backing up so that he could see both the chief and the man in black. "Don't anyone come any closer."

The man in black saw the police chief and started to back away, but Tom came up behind him and flashed his badge. The man looked resigned and put his hands on his head.

This seemed to make Max even more anxious, and I could feel his body become even more rigid. He suddenly pulled out his letter opener and put it against my neck. "Everyone, stop moving, or I'll hurt her."

Tom and the chief immediately froze.

The chief soothed, "Now, Max, you don't want to hurt anyone else. Why don't you put the knife down, and we can talk?"

I could feel the letter opener digging into my throat, and the urge to cough was almost overwhelming, but I knew if I did, it would drive the knife into my throat. I saw Tom signal something to the chief, but I didn't really understand what it was. Just then, the town's tornado alert system went off. The sound was deafening, and I realized we were standing right under one of the sirens. Max instinctively dropped his arm just enough for me to push it out of the way and try to run to Tom. Max caught the back of my shirt, but before he could drag me back, the chief had his gun trained on him.

"Don't move, or I'll shoot, and I can't miss at this range," he said with steel in his voice.

Tom pulled me away from Max, and he lowered the knife.

———————— ❧ ————————

Chapter Thirty-Seven

The next few minutes were a blur, as more police arrived and both men were handcuffed and taken off to jail. I was sitting on a log with a blanket wrapped around me. I was shivering uncontrollably, but I wasn't sure if my fever had gone back up or if it was from the adrenaline still coursing through me. Finally, things seemed to settle down, and both Tom and Chief Andrews came and stood next to me.

Before they could ask me anything, I stood up shakily and said, "Come with me. I need to show you something."

I started toward the bridge before they could object, and they both followed me. I headed straight for the falls and again went to the steps and reached in to pull out the plastic box. Both men seemed startled to see it there, and I opened it carefully. Inside, just as I suspected, was a flash drive. Before I could pull it out, the chief reached down and took the whole box from me and put it in an evidence bag.

"There might be fingerprints on the drive," he explained. "We need to preserve the evidence. Now, how did you figure out that was there?"

"A long time ago, when our daughter was young, my husband and I used to take her geocaching. We didn't have a lot of money, and it was a way to do something fun with her for free. Since we enjoyed finding the caches so much, we decided to put a few in the area that we could check on periodically. This was one of our caches. After he died, I stopped checking them, and I really thought they were probably gone. But this morning, I learned that on the morning she died, Natalie was in the park, acting like she was afraid she was being followed. She stopped here to tie her shoes, which made me wonder." Between the exertion of the walk over to the falls and all the talking, my cough was back, and I had to pause in my explanation until I could breathe again.

"Then Noelle told me someone had been talking about finding this cache a few weeks ago when Natalie and Tara were in getting coffee. I'd been trying to figure out where she might have hidden the drive, and I just knew then that this had to be it. Unfortunately, I didn't think the person following me would approach me when I was surrounded by so many other people. Just as I started to check it, I heard something, so I put it back in its hiding place. I assume you already know the rest, since I was on the phone with Tom the whole time."

They both concurred, and Tom took my hand to help me up.

Chief Andrews said kindly, "Why don't you go get some rest? I'm sure I'll have more questions later, but I think we can be done for now." He patted my shoulder gently and murmured something in Tom's ear before walking away.

"Come on," Tom said. He was still holding my hand as he began leading me up to the parking area. "My car is right here. I'll give you a lift home."

I smiled wearily and followed him back to his car.

He opened the door, helped me in, and then leaned over and looked me in the eye. "You scared me to death out there today. Once you feel better, we need to talk."

His words made me feel a little breathless with anticipation, but I simply smiled up at him. As we drove back to the house, I laid my head back against the leather seats and sighed. All the adrenaline and what little energy I had were completely gone. I closed my eyes just for a moment...

The next thing I knew, I was waking up in my bed at Lisa's to the smell of chicken soup. Lisa and Mike were standing by the side of the bed with a tray for me. It smelled like heaven.

After Lisa settled the tray in front of me, I asked, "How did I get back up here to bed? The last thing I remember is being in Tom's car on our way back here."

"Tom called me to let me know what had happened, so I was here when you got back." Mike chuckled. "None of us could wake you up, so Tom carried you up to your room, and Lisa helped get you settled."

I was sure my face had turned bright red. "I wasn't too heavy for him to carry?" I cringed at the thought of him trying to lift my deadweight up the stairs.

"He didn't seem to have any problems," Lisa answered, smiling knowingly. "In fact, it seemed effortless to me. You know, you have been losing weight, and with everything going on around here lately, you've hardly been eating. Haven't you noticed how loose your clothes are?"

I was doubtful that it was effortless, but she was right about my clothes being loose. Maybe I'd have to go visit Someone Else's Closet and get some new things. I finished eating my soup and closed my eyes as Lisa and Mike left the room.

The next day, I stayed in bed all day, miserably sick. Tom called to check on me and told me he and the chief would come by the next day to fill me in on everything.

Thankfully, I was much better when I woke up, so I took a shower, changed out of my pajamas, and had even eaten real food before they came by. We all gathered in the living room, and Tom started the explanations.

"My case involved a large drug cartel that we suspected was using cryptocurrency to launder its money. Our investigation indicated that a group of lawyers was mixing drug transactions with their clients' cryptocurrency payments to hide their origin. We started to suspect Max after a large client noticed something off about the amount in their client wallet. Apparently, Max had decided to help himself to some of their funds in addition to laundering the cartel's money."

"That's like that true crime show I watched that got me thinking about cryptocurrency." I looked at Mike and Lisa, who nodded, clearly remembering our conversation about it after I'd watched it. "So, was what I found his actual pass phrase for the crypto wallet he was using to do the money laundering?" I couldn't believe he had left it where someone could get it.

Tom said, "We think so. Still working on getting warrants to access the account, but we'll know for sure in a few days."

"And Natalie must have been the one to take it when she took the flash drive. I'm under the impression that something Natalie heard on the phone made her suspicious. At least, that was what she told Tony."

Tom nodded. "It looks like she went through Max's office and took the private key to his crypto wallet and the flash drive showing client transactions. Then she called our office. I met with her briefly in town, but she didn't have the drive with her, so we set up a time for her to meet me in the park to hand over the evidence."

"But I thought you said you didn't know anything about the drive."

"I didn't at that time. I just knew she had some evidence. It wasn't until you told me about the missing flash drive that I figured out that must be what she was planning to give me," he clarified.

"Did you have any idea she was in danger? I can't understand why she didn't just go straight to get the evidence and take you with her."

"I don't think she was in danger until Max noticed the flash drive was gone and suspected she had taken it. She didn't think he suspected her when she talked to me, and she didn't want to make him suspicious by being late getting home, so she didn't think waiting until the next day would be a problem. Something must have changed, because he followed her the next morning."

"And when she noticed she was being followed, she pretended to tie her shoe and instead stashed the drive in the geocache where I found it." I shook my head at the waste of such a vibrant young woman. "So, what were you doing out of town those days?" I asked. "If you were pursuing Max, then why leave when he was here?"

Tom grimaced. "I figured out that it couldn't have been Max who took a shot at us, which meant the cartel was at least aware that the records were missing and had sent someone here. I left to coordinate the arrests of the key cartel members in the US who were working with Max. Unfortunately, there was one left behind here."

Chief Andrews took up the narrative then. "The man you called 'the man in black' was very willing to talk to us, since he really hadn't committed any serious crimes that we could prove. He put the warning on your car, shot the light out above the two of you, and tried to break in here more than once." The chief looked at Mike. "He was very impressed with your security and very frustrated he couldn't get to Ellen to find out what she knew."

"Was he also the one watching my house?" I asked.

"Yes, but Max was the one who broke in first. He became convinced that you must have found the flash drive, and he broke in to look for it. The man in black saw him enter. Once Max left, he went in and wrote the warning."

"They both broke in! Oh my gosh!" I couldn't believe it.

"But why did they put the warning on my car?" I asked. "Without that, I might have quit looking into things. But once I was threatened, I felt like I had to keep pursuing it or be looking over my shoulder forever."

The Chief answered, "According to Vincent – your man in black – he knew you had found the body and he saw you go to the police station earlier that day when you brought me the note. He thought if he scared you, you would stop looking into things, and he could focus on Max. Once he realized that his plan backfired, he decided to keep you off balance in the hopes that you would keep pushing forward. By that point, he had heard the flash drive was missing, and he thought you had the best chance of finding it." He smiled, "And of course he was right about that."

We all laughed. We talked a bit more, but I felt like I finally had the full picture. The chief excused himself to head back to his office, and Lisa and Mike left the room to start dinner, leaving Tom and me alone.

He sat down next to me on the couch and took my hand. "Ellen, I'm going to have to leave again tomorrow to work on compiling all the evidence in this case. It may take me a few months to finish up, but a lot of that time, I can work remotely from here. I've come to really like it here in Cascade, and I think I might want to settle here for my retirement. You intrigue me like no woman I've met before, so when I get back, do you think we could go on a proper date where no one is trying to shoot at us?"

I felt overwhelmed, flattered, and overflowing with emotions. I pulled myself together enough to respond, "I'd like that a lot."

The future was looking pretty bright at the moment. A possible new job *and* a potential new relationship? I had a lot to look forward to.

The End

A Note From Jill

Thank you for spending time in Cascade with Ellen and Louisa. Writing this story was a joy, and knowing you stayed all the way to the end means more to me than I can say. Ellen has lived in my head for a long time. I'm so glad she finally gets to live in yours too.

How Ellen and Louisa Found Each Other

Before the mysteries began, there was a muddy stray dog at the end of the driveway.

"Finding Louisa" is a free prequel short story about the day Ellen's family took in the dog who would change everything. It's warm, a little bit funny, and close to my heart.

Join my readers' circle and I'll send it straight to your inbox. You'll also be the first to know when the next Ellen Douglas mystery is ready. I promise not to clutter your inbox. Just occasional notes from me, and a free story to say thank you for being here.

Scan for your free story:

*jillbrownauthor
.com/free-story*

Acknowledgements

Thank you to my editor, Jenny Rarden, and those who read the various versions of this book. Without your constructive comments and attention to detail, this book would not have been possible.

Would You Leave a Review?

Reviews are how small books like this one find their way to new readers. If you enjoyed your time in Cascade, even a sentence or two on Amazon would mean the world to me and would help other cozy mystery lovers find Ellen and Louisa.

Scan to leave a review:

*jillbrownauthor
.com/review*

Thank you. Truly.

Ellen and Louisa Will Return

"An Accidental Murder," the next Ellen Douglas mystery, arrives Fall of 2026. When the holidays bring the whole town together, they also bring old secrets to the surface, and Ellen discovers that not every accident is quite what it seems.

Want to know the moment it's available? Join the readers' circle at **jillbrownauthor.com.**

About Jill

Jill Brown spent 37 years working for the federal government before turning her attention to the kind of stories she loves most: cozy mysteries set in small towns where everybody knows everybody and somebody is usually keeping a secret. She lives in central Indiana with her husband, and spends her free time reading, playing board games, and throwing stones at her local curling club. *Murder in Cascade* is her debut novel.